Praise for
The Crazed Wind

The Crazed Wind is an ambitious, cleverly crafted work. It sweeps through important, timely topics such as displacement and rootlessness, through the eyes of the narrator and her family's experiences across decades in India and England. The core relationship between a daughter and her father is examined with psychological astuteness that lends itself to compassion towards both. Finally, by using a hybrid of fiction with elements of non-fiction, prose poetry, and playful structures, Ghosh creates an entertaining, unexpected series of pieces that blend to create a whole greater than the sum of its parts.

~ Stephanie Hutton, author of *Three Sisters of Stone*

In *The Crazed Wind*, an ostracised woman returns to India where she is reunited with her father. While the monsoon rains pour, their family history unravels in flashes addressing the differences in cultural identity and expectations with a precision and wonderment that doesn't shy away from complexity. This is a compelling and utterly absorbing portrait of a family in all its ugliness and beauty. With *The Crazed Wind* Ghosh has not only written an exemplary novella-in-flash, but one where every story stings the way flash should.

~ Santino Prinzi, author of *There's Something Macrocosmic About All of This*

As always with flash at its best, the power is in the space between the words. In *The Crazed Wind*, Ghosh provides a lush, unique collection of flash fiction that takes the reader from past to present day India and back again. The reader is taken on a turbulent journey through cultural and family divides, and is left with a disquieting truth.

~ Eileen Merriman, author of *Pieces of You* and *Catch Me When You Fall*

It's hard to pick out a few of my favorite stories without copying the table of contents but I recommend reading it straight through and take note of these stories: 'They Have a Different Heaven', 'Bhagubhai's Thumb', 'Differences', 'Fireflies'—the narrator visiting her father after ten years of strife between them, 'Sisters'—my vote for the most charming story in the novella, 'May I Introduce My Daughter?'—with this section of a paragraph which carries this painful theme throughout, *"We have always had a difficult relationship. He tried to mould my sister and me into the women he wanted us to be. When he didn't succeed, he cast us away, as if by doing so a pair of better daughters might come along and take our places."*

This is a 'must read' book so do yourself a favor, buy two—one to lend or give as a gift and the other for you to go back to time after time and read stories by choice or by chance.

Ghosh's writing combined with her story telling ability is a rare treat.

~ Paul Beckman, author of *Peek* and *Kiss Kiss*

the crazed wind

nod ghosh

TRUTH SERUM PRESS

ISBN: 978-1-925536-58-4

Truth Serum Press
32 Meredith Street
Sefton Park SA 5083
Australia

Email: truthserumpress@live.com.au
Website: https://truthserumpress.net
Truth Serum Press catalogue: https://truthserumpress.net/catalogue/

Also available as an eBook
ISBN: 978-1-925536-59-1

Truth Serum Press is a member of the
Bequem Publishing collective
http://www.bequempublishing.com/

To the memory of those
who were lost on both sides

Contents

1   They Have a Different Heaven

4   The Jewel in the Crown

5   Fundamental Differences

6   The Monsoon Began on a Wednesday

8   Annapurna

10   The Porch Swing

13   Bhagubhai's Thumb

16   Pissaap

17   Differences

19   Load Shedding

21   This is What We Learn at School Part One

22   Weather

24   Thumbprint

27   Train

29   Incomplete Lotus

31   Fireflies

36   Two Nations

37   The Perambulator

38   Sisters

40   When Girls Go Bad

41   This is What We Learn at School Part Two

43   Friends

44   Umnath

46   Matryoshka

50   May I Introduce My Daughter?

53   Immigrants or Ex-pats?

55   When She-Birds Leave the Nest
56   This is What We Learn at University
58   Discarded Fruit
60   Between Meals
61   This is What We Learn at the Workplace Part One
62   The Thickening of Blood
67   This is What We Learn at the Workplace Part Two
70   Ambition
73   The Basket
77   Talking too Much
80   Heaven Street
83   Two Gross Packages
89   Bearwood
91   My Father's Medicine Part One
93   The Bejewelled Woman on the Cover
98   Scissor Cuts
100   Harborne High Street
102   Haunted by Dream Fathers
105   Shadow
108   Super 8 Camera
111   The One In Which My Dream Father is a Duck
112   The Girl They Left Behind.
114   A Girl Named Prayer
117   Moving to a Better Place
118   O
120   The Knot in the Cream Sari
123   Unused Currency
126   Kopal
128   Garden of Eden Park
132   My Father's Medicine Part Two
134   One Night
135   Swimming

They Have A Different Heaven

He takes me to a dream from the past. "Not all dreams are good," my father warns. "Are you sure you want to come?"

We walk in parallel lines. The dust from the road burns my feet, though I'm not really here, because I haven't yet been born.

It is August 1946.

We walk past shop fronts open and looted. The air is smoky and silent. He is tall but his slight build speaks of hunger. He tells me he used to fight his brothers for scraps of food. Now he is eighteen he fights to feed the younger ones. He ventures out to find milk for crying nieces when no one else dares.

"Wait for me, Daddy," I call out. "I'll help you."

"You? What can *you* do?"

Even in this dreamscape, where heroic actions are filtered clean, there is space for a father's derision.

His stride lengthens. I run to keep up. My sandalled feet slip and twist on the rubble.

A dead dog lies tucked against a shop front, its dun fur matted with yesterday's blood. I wonder if anyone ever loved it.

We keep walking.

The stench of uncollected rubbish mingles with something more sinister.

"Don't walk so fast," I say, clutching at my father's dhuti, "why is all this happening?"

He talks about a call for a day of direct action, how antagonism between Hindu and Muslim has intensified and spilled into the streets. I struggle to hear him through the thick air.

And still we keep walking.

The city has come to a standstill, with ongoing strikes in shops and factories. There are shortages and the Black Market thrives.

"But why?" I ask. "Why are they doing this? What do they want?"

"Follow me and you'll find out."

He turns a corner and becomes younger. There are remnants of sunshine on his skin, his hair, even though the dusk has turned the ground a midden brown. I follow the boy who is to become my father.

"Jao," he commands. *Go.* The cracked bell of his childlike voice is unfamiliar. "Baritay phhirayjao." *Go back home.* All around us, the remnants of bloodshed broadcast their warning to echo his.

My father turns to face me. I am the elder, but he is the wiser one.

"Why are they doing this?" I hope he'll understand my broken words.

"Fundamental differences," he says. Once again he is an old man. Angry folds of skin vibrate around his jowls. "They fail to understand one another."

He could be talking about another time, another place.

❖

My father takes his car keys from his pocket, opens the door of the Maruti van.

"Step inside," he says. "It's getting dark. It's not safe out there." He's sitting at the wheel, keys in the ignition, ready to leave.

"But I need to understand."

"You don't need to understand. You just need to listen."

I shrink to fit inside the van, a youth, criminal in my ignorance of what has passed before, ambivalent toward the danger. I want to see what happens. I want to know what death smells like. But instead I am cocooned in metal.

"You were going to tell me why they were fighting." My voice is petulant.

"It's complex and yet it's simple," he says as we drive along the potholed road.

"I want to understand."

"You won't be able to."

"Try."

"They have a different heaven," he says, as if that is sufficient explanation.

The Jewel in the Crown

The jewel in the crown of the Empire has been lost. If anyone has seen it, send your answers in on a postcard. The battle has been won at a cost, but now the contestants have fled.

It is August 15th, 1947.

Lords and Ladies in fur coats and golden slippers, no longer summoned to dine by the dimming of the light, must gather their skirts and take flight.

Don't follow them out of the room, lest they leave a blemish, a stain, to mark this — the greatest and the worst of times.

Fundamental Differences

I gave you the best of everything, my time, my honour and my life's blood. I wanted you to soar above all others, beneath only the sky, and nothing else.

I grew like an etiolated plant without light under the oppression of your sky.

You had all the opportunities I was denied. You had the best money could buy. You had books to learn from, and a steady source of light to glean the knowledge. You had nutritious food in your belly. How could you throw everything away?

I couldn't become you. You could not see the world through my eyes, anymore than I could yours.

We sent you to the best schools. You were protected from the lower elements of society. Yet that is what you gravitated towards, to people like yourself, people who are rotten to the core.

We are different. I judge a person's worth in a different way from how you do.

I wanted to be proud of you.

I wish you had been proud of me.

What have you ever done to make me proud of you?

I've been me. I have been myself. That should have been enough, and it never was.

The Monsoon Began
on a Wednesday

I'd only been there a day. Entering the unfamiliar rooms of my father's villa, I knew I was treading uncharted ground.

The glassy air dulled my senses. I paced around like a caged dog, seeking respite from the humidity. The obliterating winds turned to rain.

Water collected in sheets and washed sections of adjacent farmland from green to grey. Palm fronds lashed in the storm, beating the air into a tight froth. The wind lifted its arms when the first thunderclaps came. The sky tugged at mango trees threatening to uproot them.

It had been years since I'd last visited.

I hadn't ever wanted to come again.

Frivolous gusts blew through the annals of my mind, and I catalogued the events that had brought me where I was. Censoring the worst parts, I saw myself in a better light. The passage of time can do that to a person.

Some say there is madness in a wind like this. It turns rich men into paupers, kings into devils. It causes skin to bubble into boils, witches to rise from misty swamps and generations of women to lose unborn babies. Some say it is the tension that builds before the event that makes these things happen. Others say it's just the badness of the world that would have come out anyway. Some say there is respite when clouds release their heavy contents. Others say it brings no relief, only that the madness keeps on building.

The gale blew through the wrought iron bars and rattled the windows. Spots of rain beat a tattoo on the greening glass.

That night, I couldn't sleep. My mind buzzed with peripheral information, tossed between different time zones, like a cup in the ocean.

I sank into the flooded abyss. The void was inundated with indigo-white water. Wading through pools that ate into the foundations of my father's house, I found the bones of my ancestors scattered in the wet dirt.

When I awoke, I knew things would never be the same between us.

Annapurna

I woke from the second dream with an overwhelming sense of loss. Insomnia and international travel had thwarted my best efforts to sleep the night before. I'd tried but failed to stay awake while my father had his afternoon nap.

But daytime sleep was always hard on me. It left me with a sense of unease and an odd taste in my mouth.

The clink of crockery and a shuffling from the floor below announced Annapurna's arrival. I pushed my fingers over my eyes.

It was the first time in years I'd come to the land where my ancestors' ashes lay. No matter where on the planet our family members went, they ended up back here. My late mother's remains had been transported from the Black Country to be scattered in the Holy Ganges.

I should have been at peace. Yet all I wanted was to go home.

Annapurna padded into my room with tea in a china cup.

Cha ennayshi.

She spoke with quiet restraint, as if she shouldn't be speaking at all. She looked at her feet, and I gazed at my own. Our eyes failed to meet.

My father's servant had an accent that came from somewhere further to the east. Annapurna, her husband and daughter worked for my father in Bagaanabad. She had other children back home. They were younger than the sun-faced girl who dusted the rooms in the hollow house.

Akhono brishti porchay.

It's still raining.

My British sensibilities led me to talk about the weather.

Annapurna didn't reply. How do you reply to absurdity? Of course it was bloody raining. It would rain for days. It would rain until every field flooded and small brown mushrooms sprang up through ruined lawns.

The pounding ballast of water on the metal roof competed with the asymmetric whir of the ceiling fan, filling out any quiet space in the room. The fan wobbled from side to side completing its wild circuit. If a blade had come away, it would potentially have decapitated Annapurna. Or me.

I asked if my father has awoken from his siesta.

She gestured and signalled, as though she had used up her quota of words for the day.

Ki, Othayni? I entreated her to speak.

Ayto, aakhon cha neay jaachhi. Annapurna gave me a professional glare. The sideways tilt of her head reinforced what she said. She was on her way to wake my father with a cup of tea. The silent subtext that followed said she should be trusted with her duty.

Annapurna shuffled down the spiral staircase, wraith-like and insignificant in her cream-coloured sari.

The flavour of scorched milk played on the root of my tongue.

The Porch Swing

My father rubbed the sleep from his eyes and I was afraid he might rub his smile away with it. The wind cut around corners, whistling like a petulant child. A momentary glimpse of sun strained through the clouds and cast shadows around our swaying legs.

"Your mother and I used to sit here for hours," he said. "She loved the swing seat."

"Maybe because you can see the garden from here." I sipped on the thick tea that reminded me of sweetened condensed milk, careful not to spill any onto the floral fabric of the swing.

"She loved the garden." He shifted his gaze away from me, glanced at the swaying trees.

"She could make anything grow. Do you remember her Swiss cheese plant in England? You had to leave it in the house when you sold it, didn't you? It was too big to move."

"That plant was like a child to her."

We both know there is no answer to that, because my mother was deprived of her actual children for over a decade.

We'd spoken of my mother's love of plants at her funeral. My sister had included it in the order of service. She'd initially mistyped "plants", missed out the letter "L". We had howled with laughter at her error, three siblings semi-orphaned, getting pissed on chardonnay, giggling like maniacs, tears streaming down our faces, while our father the widower slept upstairs.

The memory dimmed and flickered and I fought to fix my smile. It was hard not to frown when I remembered my mother's forced exile. She'd been isolated, spent her days tending to plants in her paradise prison, the sprawling villa I was visiting in Bagaanabad, east of Kolkata.

My father had taken her with him when he announced he wanted nothing to do with us; first my sister, then me.

I'd visited her in what I called the mausoleum before. I'd snuck into the villa when my father had been in hospital.

My father's expectations had kept my mother apart from two of her three children for a decade. She had hoped for reconciliation. She had died hoping.

On this visit, my father and I were tentative in our interactions, both aware the fuse might ignite at any time, and that the resulting explosion might lead to the period of exile being resumed, and perhaps extend to the rest of our lives.

We discovered safety in the past.

We sat on that porch swing and talked about people from my childhood. Before misdirected career choices. Before rebellion. Before boyfriends. Girlfriends. Before making our own way in the world.

We talked about neighbours. About friends. Business acquaintances. Teachers. Idiots. Savants. We talked about family, but only those who had not been swallowed into the dark pit of disapproval where my sister and I had resided for years.

I had many questions. "Do you remember when Stan handled Thakuma's Holy shrine?" I asked.

"Yes. He was trying to clean it. Funny old man. I gave Stanley his first cigarette. I'll always regret that."

"Was there someone called Sandra that we used to visit when I was really young?"

"Yes. She was the daughter of an old friend of mine. We stayed with them a few times. Just outside London, when I was taking my dinners at Lincoln's Inn."

"And Uncle Umnath. Were we related to him, or just friends?"

"Friends."

"Like Uncle Rohin. We weren't related to him either were we? Do you remember when his daughter sent me a letter but forgot to put my name on the envelope?"

"No. I can't remember that."

"You opened it, and then told *me* off because she'd written she had a dream where I was kissing David Cassidy."

My father said nothing. But he will have remembered. He will have remembered confining me to my room for a day. I changed the subject.

"And those boys who used to help out at the warehouse, do you remember the guy who stole the honey?"

"And the two tricksters who stole all the money from the exhibition?" He was warming to the theme again.

"And Bhagubhai. Do you remember Bhagubhai?"

My father was momentarily silent. He stopped the momentum of the swing with his foot.

"No," he said. Stony. Chilled. "I don't remember anyone of that name."

Ah, but I know he did.

Bhagubhai's Thumb

When Bhagubhai cut his thumb off, my grandmother Thakuma scurried upstairs and locked herself in her room for fear of being contaminated by his blood.

Ma tut-tutted and dressed the man's hand in one of my brother's clean T-shirts, whilst I stood in the doorway biting a hangnail, praying under my breath.

Turns out Bhagubhai hadn't cut half or even a quarter of his thumb off whilst adjusting the lawnmower. The emergency department had examined the gash, Ma told us, and then stitched the thing together. I asked whether Bhagubhai had cried, but Ma said grown-ups didn't cry at such things.

There were other things grown-ups didn't do that Bhagubhai *did* do though, things that Ma, Baba and Thakuma knew nothing about.

Our house had many rooms and corridors. You could lose yourself in its spires and mazes. You could hide for a whole day, and no one would find you. It never occurred to me as a seven-year-old that the reason no one found me on those hot days was because nobody was looking.

My brother and I roamed free. We crawled through junk-filled rooms where Baba stored chairs, tables and wardrobes he'd bought at auction. Then the boy would lie with Thakuma for his afternoon nap, and I would sneak away and tap on the back window.

No one noticed the man-child employed to mow the lawns, clean the car and scrub the toilets, when he crept into the pantry to play house with me.

Bhagubhai brought treasures down from the top shelf. He poured pretend tea from Thakuma's long-spouted brass teapot. I watched his gap-toothed smile fold over his goblet's rim as we drank cupsful of syrupy air. We cut into imaginary *sandesh* and giggled until we heard Thakuma on the stairs.

He'd slip away before we were caught.

Sometimes we played hide and seek in the park across the road.

Sometimes we played counting games.

Ikri mikri chaam chikri ...

No matter how often he showed me, skirting his fingers over mine like he was playing a musical instrument, I couldn't capture the moves, or learn the words of his song.

When Bhagubhai injured his thumb, I'd already sensed things were changing.

Baba said the car didn't shine enough. Thakuma complained about unclean spirits. Nothing was fast enough, clean enough, short enough or long enough.

They questioned me. I was made to place my palm on Thakuma's, to swear to tell the truth.

Did you play together, just the two of you?

Yes.

Where did you play?

What did you play?

Yes.

No.

Yes.

I tried to give the right answers, but the wrong words jumped out of my mouth.

We played *Ikri mikri.*

Yes.

He touched me with his fingers.

When Thakuma invoked the names of several gods, I knew it was over.

Sometimes I can't sleep. I feel Bhagubhai's fingers dance over my own.

Ikri mikri chaam chikri ...

I drift off, and ask him to teach me the words.

But he never does.

Pissaap

A mother holds her infant over a drain at the side of the road and makes a urinary hiss through her lips until the girl, less than a year in age, voids her bladder.

She hoists the child up, and folds her into the sling of her sari.

Differences

When I am a child, you tell me a husband should be chosen with care.

I say I'll never marry, because I hate boys.

When I am older, you don't like the way I look at youths on the street.

I despise the girl's school where we are led like horses, saddled and blinkered.

When I leave home, you tell me to be careful. There are men who will use a woman and discard her.

When I leave home, I'm glad to take risks. There are men who use women, as there are women who use men.

You advise me to choose a man with impressive qualifications.

I'd be content with one who is intelligent.

You like a tall man, narrow waisted, well dressed.

I prefer one who doesn't have a narrow outlook.

You recommend men who are solid and reliable.

I want a man who will share his wildness with me.

You extol the virtues of maturity.

I want someone who will play with me.

You advise me to find someone who can tell right from wrong.

I want someone who can see what I'm doing is right, even if it is wrong.

You say life is not all fun and games.

I want someone who can make me laugh, even though I know how hard it is to be funny.

You admire men who make money.

I like a man who will make things with his hands and mind.

You would be proud to call a man who makes his mark in society your son-in-law.

I would be happy to live anonymously with love.

You respect a man who is steadfast, unafraid.

I admire a man who is not afraid to cry.

You cannot abide weakness.

Sometimes it is in weakness we discover our strength.

And though I no longer hate boys, it's not a man I want at all.

It is a woman.

Load Shedding

Rain pulverised the ground, cutting the earth like fingernails to foreign skin.

The manservant with a limp fidgeted at the entrance to my room. He said my father was calling for me. He'd summoned me to listen to his next story. The man glided down the spiral staircase with his candle.

He took his name with him.

Father was absorbed in the ritualistic consumption of tea and dry biscuits when I joined him in the parlour. A peculiar light illuminated shadows on his face. He looked like a deposed monarch. The air was thinner above his head, where his crown would have been.

"So what do you want to know?" he asked, tucking a broken piece of Rich Tea biscuit into his mouth. *Ar ki bolbo? What else can I say?* He alternated between English and Bangla.

Anything and everything, I wanted to tell him, but kept silent. I knew in time, he would continue unprompted. The lamp-flame flickered like a lost genie.

My father spoke about elections around the time of Partition. I murmured an occasional word of encouragement, otherwise remained silent. He gave me encyclopaedia perfect answers. Names. Dates. Political scandals.

"What was it like for you, though?" I asked. "What did it *feel* like to be part of that?"

"This bloody load shedding," he complained as if I hadn't spoken. The electricity had been cut off for the third time that day. He complained about city officials. He mimicked a minister bleating about crumbling infrastructure. The light from candles the limping man had ignited glistened on souvenirs from European cities that sat in a wooden cabinet.

My father continued. He spoke of voter bashing, corruption and ballot rigging, unaffected by my furious note taking. I didn't want to lose a thing.

The low light made me sleepy, and I stifled a yawn.

But my father wasn't ready to stop.

He had too much to say.

I worried about missing nuances and minor details in my scribbles. It was the details I wanted most from him.

The manservant swept into the room and cleared the cups away. My father cleared his throat, and directed the man with his forehead. He pointed to a pile of dirty plates on his desk.

It seemed they conducted most of their conversations without the benefit of words.

My father was saving his words for me.

This is What We Learn at School
Part One

History: to learn how things *really* happened and find out later that they *really* happened a different way.

Biology: to learn nature can be tamed by humans, rather than humans being at the mercy of nature.

Mathematics: to rote learn what happens when you multiply a number by another without understanding what happens when things grow out of control.

Art: to learn something that is regarded as futile and discover you like it more than anything else.

Geography: to learn about places other than here. Places you could go back to, if only that's where you had come from.

English: to make it clear you are not English, though you aren't sure what you really are.

Weather

I learned to change the weather when I was six. The process was pain-free and took less than half an hour.

When we headed to Queen's Park, I'd perform my ritual in the privacy of my bedroom or in the haven of the upstairs toilet. The procedure involved calling on guardian spirits and a choreography of complex arm movements.

By the time my mother strapped my brother into his pram and we'd buttoned our coats up, the sun would pop out from behind grey clouds.

I became reluctant to leave the house without ample warning. I needed time to switch off the wind, or wipe cotton wool tufts away from the sky.

When my grandmother's pumpkins shrank and wilted from lack of rain, I made it pour for days.

Once I made a thunderstorm just for fun.

The hail on my sister's birthday was no coincidence; and though I caused it to snow on the hills for Christmas Day, I couldn't make the white dust settle.

I became adept at meteorological manipulation.

❖

My first failure came as a shock. I commanded a rainbow and nothing came. Everything else went wrong at around the same time.

I performed poorly at school.

I forgot how to spell, especially words like "cumulus" and "Saint Swithun's".

I unlearned my times tables.

My best friend found a new best friend.

The fish died. Bees followed suit.

I'm an old lady now. It's been years since I locked myself in the bathroom and manoeuvred my arms into position to invoke the guardian spirits. They'd stopped responding. Things have gone the other way now.

It's hard to *stop* the weather from changing even though I'm not trying anymore.

Thumbprint

The wind let up for a little while that morning. When I came down the spiral staircase, my father was seated in command position in the heavily upholstered chair in his lounge.

Annapurna made a small bow as I passed her, asked if I wanted breakfast or tea. I signalled no.

A line of ragged men waited to seek an audience with my father. He wore a black suit, shirt and tie, instead of his usual dhuti. Despite the incessant rain, it was stifling and hot. I felt his skin prickle with the heat, as if I had nerves under his skin.

Aykhanay shoi koro, he commanded, thrusting a cracked ballpoint pen at the man at the front, indicating a spot on a ledger where he was required to sign his name.

I sat in silence, picked up the book about Albert Einstein I'd found on his bookshelf the day before, and pretended to read.

The man shuffled out of the room, eyes averted as he passed me.

I understood these were the men who would be working on the construction site at the front end of the compound. My father was having a block of flats built. Taller. Wider. More expansive that the block that housed the unit he already occupied. No one lived in the rest of the building he was in, although a family resided in a hut near the gazebo at the back of the property.

The men arrived every day to work. Many of them lived in the poorer part of Bagaanabad near the railway tracks. They brought the smell of the trains with them.

I cast my eyes down on the book, but kept the men in the periphery of my consciousness. The words in the Einstein biography were as incomprehensible as they had been the day before.

Aykhanay shoi koro, my father commanded the next man.

He twisted his head from side to side in the way Indian people do, that can mean yes, no or maybe.

My father opened an inkpad and the man pushed his thumb into it. He pressed his digit into the ledger, rocked it back and forth and crept out of the room to join his co-workers.

When the last worker left the room, my father closed the ledger and patted the seat next to him, signalling me to sit by his side.

"Kajal telephoned earlier," he said by way of greeting.

"Is she coming to visit?" I hoped my cousin would come, to lighten the heaviness that came from treading cautiously for several days. It was easy to annoy my father, even easier to send him into paroxysms of rage. Having another person present diffused the situation.

"She'll be here in time for lunch," he replied, and something danced inside my chest. I looked at my watch. It was still early. I counted the hours.

Setting Einstein down on the coffee table, I stepped into the courtyard where the men were chatting, smoking beedis, laughing, unconcerned by the diagonal rain that soaked into their clothes.

Ay, chhati, chhati. Annapurna scuttled after me waving an umbrella.

I twisted my head from side to side in the way Indian people do. It could have meant yes, or no. It could have meant maybe.

Train

I must be less than five years old. It's before I've started school.
I have a sister, but no brother. He's not born yet.

We wait in line to go on the model railway ride. Everyone's
staring. They always do. It could be the white tulle party dresses
my sister and I wear. It could be my mother's sari. It might be
our skin.

A girl and boy jiggle near the queue of people. They could
have walked out from an Enid Blyton novel. They are drawn to
the little train that toots its pious little horn. They want to be
where we are. You can tell by the way they hold themselves.
They each take one step nearer, one step back, like they're
doing a dance.

"Are you coming on the train?" my father asks, making a
space for them.

"Ain't got no money, Mister," the boy says.

It doesn't occur to me to question what they are doing here,
with their sky-blue shorts, ice-cream-with-freckles complexions
and no money. Their jumping and skipping. Their lemonade
smiles.

We've reached the front of the queue. It's time to pay.

"I'll get your tickets," Dad says. "Climb on board."

"Gosh!" the boy does a little jump.

"Gee, mister," the girl says.

The boy and the girl sit next to my father, opposite my sister and me. I hold my mother's hand. The folds of my party dress under my thighs stop me from sticking to the painted wooden seat.

The train chugs away, but I'm not looking at the trees, the monkey swings, the river with a bridge on it. I'm not looking at the cages, the lake.

I look at the boy and the girl. I cut my lip with my teeth to stop a smile from escaping. I'll do anything so I don't have to speak to them, I'm that shy. My sister's the same. We look at each other and look away again. An animal shrieks in the distance and then the train grinds to a halt.

The girl and boy don't say a thing. No thank you, no please, no nothing.

The boy unclips the catch on the door and runs to a waiting group of children. They have the same bovine smiles. Some wear shorts, some wear skirts. They all have flat pockets.

"That blackie there paid for our ride!" The girl points a finger. It is a finger of accusation, a finger that might go searching for a bogey later when it's time for tea.

My father's smile fades to a whisper of shame.

"Come on," our mother says. "Let's go and see the boats."

I avoid looking over my shoulder as we leave the train.

The children's laughter echoes into the canopy of trees above us.

Like monkeys.

Incomplete Lotus

A membrane of petal-thin paper threatens to disintegrate. I take out photographs stamped with the credentials of a studio in Kolkata, and a family tree that spans eleven generations. Names stripped from flesh and bone.

There are birth dates and places I have never known: Binnaguri to Bikrampur. Sepia images. A tea stain diffuses from my grandfather's shoulder. The turn of his lips is mirrored in my own face.

A bride with vermillion sindoor markings pouts from 1925. A crease in the photograph separates the girl from her husband. Her name is Prativa. She was born in 1912. I shudder to think she is my flesh. I weep when I think of her blood.

I use these fragments to weave a canopy for my children, to cushion them from rootlessness. Relics that anchor them to a past none of us know. I use a protractor to measure degrees of separation from Indians seen in history books. I use callipers to calculate the distance from a great grandmother's embrace.

Then there is the story that transcends dates and lineage. It happens in the 1930s. Prativa embroiders a lotus flower, bright colours on black cloth. She works late into the night, children asleep, stitches in and out of fabric pulled taught across a frame. Her children share a bed beside her. The oil lamp's glow illuminates her fingers in their industry. She pokes her tongue between thin lips and licks a thread. A light breeze stirs the stifling heat.

Prativa works for months between feeds and cleaning. She works for years, after bathing and before preparing her husband's meal. When the needlework is almost complete, she stops. She leaves one lotus petal unfilled, a challenge to future daughters-in-law. *You have to finish this work.*

Then Prativa puts the incomplete lotus away, a puzzle with a missing piece, an heirloom in the making. She sets the challenge to her sons, not her daughters.

"What happened to it?" I ask my uncle through crackles and crossed lines.

"To what?" The difference in our time zones is a window that separates his here and my now.

"The lotus. Did anyone ever finish it?"

"No," he says. "No one ever dared."

Fireflies

I have never seen a firefly before, but this night is full of surprises. The air is hot and spicy, shrill with the sound of insects calling to mates, anxious screeches with tinny replies.

I arrived at my father's house four days ago. He and I face an uneasy truce after a decade of discord. This evening we have mains electricity, though the power is often cut after five.

My cousin Kajal has spent the day here. We've walked through saturated grounds and gathered bunches of monsoon flowers, cutting the stems with my mother's old penknife. The blooms look like gladioli, white and gorgeous with spiky leaves. Kajal had shaken water off their heads. Her movements remind me of my dead mother, though she is related through my father's side.

Her presence dilutes the tension between my father and me. He has insisted Kajal stay overnight. The road to Kolkata is potholed and lined with vagrants, he says. It's not safe to take a taxi back to the city at this hour, or so he says. Kajal knows this is nonsense, but doesn't contradict her uncle. He is a difficult man to disobey. Though there are countless rooms in this building that I call the mausoleum, he has arranged for my cousin to sleep in the bed next to mine.

"You'll have a lot to talk about after so long," he says, and he is right.

❖

My cousin moved to England when I was three. She joined our family in quiet suburbia. Kajal studied and married there. She stayed until her divorce.

She had been stylish and elegant. With her husband, Kajal entertained smart people in bright soirées; musicians, artists and writers. It all ended when the husband left her for one of the smart friends. Now my cousin spends half the year in India, half in the U.K., where her children are.

Kajal hesitates when we walk up the spiral staircase to the room we will share.

"Oh," she says inexplicably. "He put us here." There's sadness to her voice.

"You can sleep somewhere else if you want," I offer. "I'll ask Annapurna to make up one of the other beds."

"No," she says. "I *want* to sleep here. I feel — I feel closer — "

My cousin doesn't finish her sentence. She lays her case on the bed next to the one I'm using, throws a mosquito net over the framework and seals the inner chamber by tucking the overhang under the mattress.

A bar of light projects from under my father's door into the corridor between his room and ours. Kajal and I wait until it is extinguished before we close ourselves into the room, to light up our first cigarette.

"Okay if I share?" I ask. "Don't know if I can manage a whole one."

32

Kajal nods, draws on the greenish beedi, holds the smoke in her lungs and passes the glowing stick to me without a word.

I'm in my forties and Kajal even older, yet we still enjoy the thrill of a clandestine cigarette. My father will likely smell the smoke, and join in the game, pretending not to notice. We chat in semi-hoarse whispers, afraid the sound will carry.

"Hey look over there," Kajal says after lighting another. She clicks the lamp off and the incandescent glow from the second cigarette transforms her face to a ghostly orange.

"See?" She nudges me, lifts my hand and directs it towards the window.

I don't see them at first. My eyes are not accustomed to the gloom. But when I do, I wonder how Kajal saw them when the lights were on, and how I *didn't* once the lamp went out. The blunt green glow of two fireflies dancing their schizophrenic waltz is fascinating. They dart across the room. The faint rustling sound beside me indicates Kajal has turned her head to follow their flight.

"Some people say they are the souls of departed loved ones," she says.

An adult firefly only lives for three to four weeks. They live long enough to mate and produce eggs. It is thought that they consume pollen or nectar, though it's possible they eat nothing at all in their adult stage; a brief existence with an appetite only for sex.

The next morning I tell Annapurna and her daughter about the fireflies. The young girl helps her mother around the house by dusting the many empty rooms. She tells us about the festival float her friends and family made a year ago. They collected thousands of fireflies, plucked their glowing rear ends off and glued them to the wooden effigies that were paraded through the street.

They won a prize for the best display.

I am horrified. No one else understands my distaste, my sympathy for the small soulless creatures, or my abhorrence at their dying chemiluminescence.

The girl smiles in gap-toothed nonchalance.

Mounting the spiral staircase, I find Kajal bent by the side of the bed. At first I think she's praying. Her hands are clasped together in forlorn supplication. But I know that's unlikely. Kajal is as religious as a ham sandwich laced with gin. Tears push through the corners of her closed lids. I hardly dare breathe, ashamed of my bitter intrusion.

My cousin turns to face me.

"This it where it happened," she says.

"What?"

"Here in this room."

Uncertain what she's referring to, I kneel next to Kajal and take her hand.

"What happened?"

"This is where my mother died."

I realise what it means for Kajal to be in this part of the mausoleum.

That night, after Kajal has left, two fireflies dance in the darkness when I blow my candle out. Years ago, my mother phoned me to say she had found her sister-in-law's body, lifeless on the bed, in this room inside this immense house. She'd cried when she told me.

I try to believe the light represents my aunt's liberated soul.

But I know they are only insects lost in a frenzy of love before death.

Two Nations

Let's celebrate the birth of two nations. Let's rejoice at liberation. Let's hold up the doctrine of non-violence for the entire world to see. Let us sing soaring anthems till our throats are raw.

Let's emulate Lords and Ladies, whose hurried departure left cracks in the landscape.

Let's not count the cost of an unclean cut, with edges too ragged and bloody to mend.

The Punjab is broken. People move in opposite directions, their destination determined by the colour of their beliefs.

Let's not see rootless children too hungry to cry, legs too thin to carry their hollow bodies. Blame individual gods who have left them to their individual fates.

Let us not speak of fathers who slice daughters' throats, to preserve their honour when the enemy arrives.

And what of Bengal, if it's mentioned at all?

And Kashmir?

The Perambulator

The mother walks proud beside her husband. The sun is a golden thing. She pushes a shiny black perambulator. Silver Cross. Beetle black.

Inside the sheltered box, an infant destined for great things.

Sisters

Sisters whisper silent rules. They haven't always been friends, and they won't always be this close.

"I am the genie of the lamp," the elder says. "I can grant your heart's desire."

"Can I have anything?" the younger girl asks, hesitant.

"Anything you want." The genie folds her hands into a prayer.

The younger child wishes for a beautiful piece of paper. Shiny. Golden. Sticky on one side.

"It is here." The older child flourishes an imaginary sheet and lays it at her sister's feet.

"Oh that's beautiful," the child says. "May I have another wish?"

"You may," the older one replies.

"I can't think what I want."

"Gold? Silver? Black diamonds?"

"Bring me all three."

The older child heaves the chest of treasure onto the floor, and between them, they try on every jewel; crowns, diadems, bangles and rings.

"May I have another wish?"

"You may. I can bring you the world's sweetest wine. Nothing finer will ever pass your lips."

The girl adjusts the embroidered cloth that is her cloak.

"Bring me wine," the younger sister replies.

The elder pours liquid, thin as air, rich as molasses, from a long-spouted brass teapot.

The younger watches the goblet fill with astonished eyes. When she drinks, her mouth bursts with the excitement of their pretence.

When Girls Go Bad

When girls go bad, they smell terrible. They spread like weeds, unkempt and dishevelled. They answer back, fail exams and mix with the wrong sort.

When girls go bad, they steal your medicine and light fires. But these are not fires that fulfil hopes or provide answers to your dreams. These girls are arsonists with a twist of chilli pepper.

When girls go bad, they destroy everything you have built, then sweep away the ashes.

Bad girls are a liability, a metal yoke around your neck. Bad girls respect no one, and fight like cannibal pirates.

It's best to nip these things in the bud. If you find your girls are starting to go off, get rid of them before it's too late.

This is What We Learn at School
Part Two

Monday. You've long since learned to tie your laces, and now you're going to different places.

Imagine yourself in the arms of someone your father would hate, someone from the lower elements of society.

Tuesday. Like the cut of someone's cloth, more than anything you own.

You close your eyes when you take cash from your mother's purse. If you don't see it, it hasn't happened.

Wednesday. Run the double-blinded mile, to emulate another's style.

There's no such thing as a new idea. But you like to make your own mind up whom to copy.

Thursday. Drinking vodka in the park. Stumbling footfall after dark, with someone you only met the once.

It's good to take a chance. Or two.

Friday. Steal your brother's mirror shades and take your father's razor blades.

Cut the stigma from your skin. Tell yourself you're not doing it because you're sad, but because you want to.

Saturday. A sheep like many in a crowd, you find you have to turn around.

The wolf is kinder than you thought, but leaves stains on your sheets and in other places.

Sunday. Your idols left you far behind. Companionship's so hard to find.

You feel a new kind of lonely. Diminished in stature. Diminished in worth. You don't want to go back to school next week.

Friends

The value of friends varies according to the currency used to measure them.

Your careless dismissal of mine used to sadden me. Yet in recent years, I am sad because you lack true friends.

You crave the protection of high walls around you, but they negate the possibility of a chance encounter, or a neighbourly chat over the fence. The metaphorical walls are even harder to scale.

You used to have friends. They were abundant in the community of migrants who found each other in a new land.

You talk about them as if they are near you, still warm, still bringing lightness and joy into your life.

I talk about them as if I believe you.

I ask about one of numerous "uncles" I grew up with.

"And Uncle Umnath. Were we related to him, or just friends?"

"Friends," you say.

And I believe you again.

Umnath

The whiteness of Umnath's bones hides beneath trembling fingers, but he scratches his shins oblivious to what's inside. He rubs until his skin becomes tomato red. His chin rests on brown-paper knees. The matchbox abrasions of his breath betray the uncertainty of diseased lungs, though those organs function better than his brain. The rattle of his breathing is a reminder of the impermanence of life. But it is the rattling of loose thoughts in moments of lucidity that tell Umnath he has lived too long.

The running. There was always the running. Long ago. The memory heightens the redundancy of his limbs.

Running. Running under the reddened sky. The sky is decimated by a blast-furnace glow. The relentless bloom of flies, the screams of children, throats tight with hunger. The kathakali dance of cicadas locked in ritual encounters. The scent of a hundred year's incense from the Gita Mandir, where dream-gods march next to sleeping ancestors. The tambour of beggar boys with bellies like drums. The disappointment of rice without meat.

Metallic fumes shorten the air. The juxtaposition of love and decay in roadside shanties. A screeching baby at its mother's breast, shocked by the enormity of its existence. Shit floating in a slow turning river. The mechanical beat of October's heat that refuses to die after nightfall. Umnath runs through all of this. It happened so long ago, and yet it is happening to him now. He runs until something tears inside his chest, and he can run no more. He stops beside a stall selling aubergines and leather handbags.

Umnath catalogues his thoughts in jumbled disorder.

He runs to a new life. The improbability of escape becomes probable. A scholarship, long years of study, the accountability of dreams.

The transference of ambition to his children. They know nothing about struggle. They know nothing about running. They hold his hand, and talk to him like he is stupid. And all he can do is stare back at them like someone who is stupid. Because that is what this disease has done to Umnath. It has made him stupid.

His son says "good day" to the man in the bed opposite, a creature with yellow skin, the tallow hue of death. He runs to a different history. The beat of his memory takes a different path.

Though he has been there for five weeks, Umnath has never spoken to the man.

He never will.

Matryoshka

They look as if they are carved from the same piece of wood, though it's clear they are not.

A teenage girl dusts between the series of interlocking Russian dolls my mother bought in 1972. The girl wears a bright orange salwar kameez and has a flower tucked behind one ear. Today is one of the first days since I arrived that she has been able to gather flowers from the grounds. It's the first day everything has not been obliterated by rain.

"We never went to Russia, did we?" I ask my father.

"Yes we did. Mum and I went once."

"But not then. Not when she got these." I wander to the shelf where the girl waves a duster in a perfunctory manner. Picking up the baby doll, I roll it in my fingers.

"Didn't we get these in Poreč?"

"Yugoslavia?" he asks, looking up at the figure.

"It's Croatia now," I add, placing the figure back between strokes of the girl's duster.

"I suppose it will be." He turns a page of his paper. "Everything changes."

"How do you mean?"

"Where I was born, the place my ancestors lived." He folds his paper and smooths it onto the coffee table. "That's Bangladesh now."

"And before that was it East Pakistan?"

"All part of India when I was a child," he says, fanning himself with a magazine.

"Tell me more about when you were a boy."

"What do you want to know?"

"Tell me about your parents, our ancestors."

"Did I ever tell you my father's name?" He is enthusiastic again. Sometimes he welcomes the opportunity to talk about the past.

"No, I only knew him as *Dadu*." I'd never had the chance to use this honorific, as I never met either of my grandfathers.

"His name was Shitul." My father smiles. "It means cool-headed."

"And was he?"

"What?"

"Cool-headed?"

"No. He had a fiery temper."

I reflect my grandfather had that in common with other family members, but keep the thought to myself.

"His older brother threw Shitul out of the family home in Shiladharchar," he continues. "We never knew why. I suppose my father must have done something unacceptable."

The relaxed manner in which he discusses his father's expulsion doesn't surprise me. Family members were ostracised then for minor misdemeanours, just as they have been in my generation. Only for us, it is mainly the girls who are disowned.

"He was thrown out of the house naked," he continues, beginning to enjoy his own story.

I have no reason to believe my father is not telling the truth, though I wonder if by "naked" he means my grandfather lacked suitable outer garments to travel, or whether he was bare-skinned.

"Later on, one of his sisters crept out of the house and gave him her own garments, so he could get away."

"Where did he go?"

"Baba was always vague about that part. He didn't return to the family home until he had completed his medical qualifications. Nobody knows how he financed his education. He may have done something illegal for all they knew."

It becomes clear why I was never told this story as a child.

The girl in the salwar kameez responds to her mother's call, and disappears from the room.

"However," my father continues, "years later, they found a case in his rooms containing thousands of locks and keys."

"So had he worked as a locksmith or something?"

"No one knows. He never told anyone."

"And now he's gone, we'll never know."

"No. We won't." He sips from the glass of lemon water the girl brought him earlier.

"Stories disappear with unfinished endings when people die, don't they?" I sip from my drink.

"Some things are lost forever."

"I won't have the chance to find out very much about Mum's family now she's gone." I'm tentative about probing further. "What do you know about them?"

"Your grandfather on that side was called Sudhish Chandra Bose." He doesn't seem unwilling to talk about her family, even though speaking about her can cause him to be visibly pained. "Pass me that picture, I'll tell you more." He points to the silver-framed photo the girl has just dusted.

48

Grandfather Sudhish is in his thirties or forties. He is a slight man with low-set ears and the same down-turned lips as I have. My father unfolds a slip of paper that is tucked inside the frame.

"His father was called Satish Chandra Bose." He pushes his glasses further down his nose and reels off a chain of ancestors. *Hari Mohan Bose, Ram Ratan Bose, Ram Jagannath Bose.*

The names nest into each other like the interlocking Russian dolls that weren't from Russia. Only these are all male.

"How do you know all this?"

"Someone did a thesis on local family ancestry, and your mum's family was included."

"What about the women? Who were my grandmother's people?"

"Oh, they only looked at the male lineage."

He is right, I think. When people die, some things are lost forever.

May I Introduce My Daughter?

My father manages to say my daughter's name.

There is power in words, and articulating someone's moniker is honouring their existence in a way.

He looks at my photographs from New Zealand and asks how she is doing at school, how she has coped with the move from the U.K. He asks why she is so skinny.

We haven't argued very much during the two weeks I've stayed with him in Bagaanabad. Our politics and religious views are similar. Our ideas on class and social standing are not.

I do not share his fixation on grooming. He tells me I dress less well than some of his servants. I take umbrage at the fact that he has people working for him he calls servants. He tells me I look uneducated. I tell him I don't wear my degree certificates sewn into the lining of my clothes. He tells me I could have done "so much better". I tell him I don't measure a person's worth by the number of certificates they collect over a lifetime, or by the money in their pockets.

He is pleased when I say my daughter wants to be a lawyer or journalist. I tell him about her hobbies and friends, but he makes it clear this information is superfluous.

The last time I came to India, I had my girl with me. She was eleven at the time and really *was* skinny then. Perhaps that's what he's remembering. We'd flown over in a hurry, because my mother had bled into her brain.

My uncle had picked us up from the airport, and informed me my father would take us to the hospital.

"But?" I'd said.

I was silenced by his words. My father was picking us up, and that was how things were going to be.

My father and I hadn't spoken to each other for eleven years.

We have always had a difficult relationship. He tried to mould my sister and me into the women he wanted us to be. When he didn't succeed, he cast us away, as if by doing so a pair of better daughters might come along and take our places.

My brother's actions were subject to a different set of rules.

This visit is different. My father holds me in his arms and smiles when I arrive. Mum isn't around any more. Though she survived the bleed, another one killed her later.

I, in turn, am eager to learn what has made him the way he is. I catch glimpses when he tells me of his life around the time of Partition. How his whole family, three brothers, three sisters and parents lived in a room the size of his current living room.

Perhaps that is why he lives in a house with several unoccupied rooms. He's still compensating.

When my father picked us up in his Maruti van, three years earlier, I stepped into the back with my girl in tow.

"Hello Dad," I said.

He said nothing.

"May I introduce my daughter?"

We drove to the hospital in silence.

My mother was woozy and disorientated.

She smiled when she saw her granddaughter, managed to say her name.

There's power in a name.

My daughter kissed my mother lightly on the cheek and told her she loved her.

Immigrants or Ex-pats?

Those Bengalis sure knew how to have a good time.

They are young and beautiful in the photograph. One of the women from the picture has scanned and uploaded it onto social media. Though well into her fifties, the woman is a five-year-old with bouncing black curls and frothy white party dress when the picture was taken. I can only guess her dress is white, not pale blue, lemon or pink. Her monochromatic smile is faithfully reproduced.

There's her father whose name I never knew. He was simply one of numerous "uncles" I grew up with.

There's power in a name.

There's Uncle Rohin. And Auntie Beena, though I'm not sure we knew her then. It might be someone who looks like her. Auntie Moina is there though. I'd never mistake her fine features, chiselled and regal, like the bird after which she is named. She's sitting on the floor next to my mother, who is round with me in her belly.

There is no sign in my mother's eyes of the pain of separation she will be feeling, and the emptiness a gathering like this must cause her. You cannot fathom the sadness she will have felt at leaving her parents behind in the insane green of her homeland. You cannot see the distress she swallows in forced mouthfuls, at being away from her friends, tangerine skies, and the shiny black perambulator that holds her eldest daughter.

Oh but who's that playing the sitar? His name dances to the forefront of my brain, willing me to remember it. He's sitting next to Uncle Umnath. Auntie Krishna pushes a mound of sugary confection into the man's mouth.

Underneath the bubble-haired girl's post, my brother has commented *why are we called immigrants, yet when the Brits go overseas, they are called ex-pats?*

When She-Birds Leave the Nest

They fly with enthusiastic caution, jumping over the edge to leave the safe haven they have called home most of their lives. They launch one at a time and don't look back. They haven't been pushed, but it is clear when it's time for the she-birds to go.

They skirt around the vicinity, preening their dull brown plumage, scratching in the earth to capture an unlikely meal; a worm, a beetle, the occasional itinerant who's hard on his luck and is looking for a good time.

A squawk from the resident fledgling becomes quieter and quieter still, the farther the girls move from the nest they once called home.

This is What We Learn
at University

On the first day, we are shy finches, camouflaged against the autumnal urban decay. We hunch our shoulders to hide our spotted plumage, pushing through hoards of sparrows united in their dull plumage of sweatshirt and jeans. The movements in every direction are enough to make us feel sick. We stride on, our faces bent away from the cruel north wind, feet soaked in puddling rain.

It's hard to speak to so many new voices all at once.

There are forms to fill in, keys to cut, and locks to open.

Crisp laundered linen in hostels smells different from the sheets we know. The ceilings are high, but rents are low.

In the evening, we follow the parade of penguins, geese and graduate students to the bar, where we practice drinking and perfect our smoking skills. There are paper tickets in our welcome packs that allow us entry into halls where the music is loud enough to make our bellies vibrate.

An ostrich with matching moustache and tail feathers tries to buy us drinks, the cut of his trousers as unimpressive as the timbre of his mating call. We separate around him like migrating starlings.

❖

When sufficient beer has been consumed, the dance begins. Peacock feathers, erect and ostentatious, impress us so easily. These birds are replete with knowledge about which rock bands to like and which to hate. The cocks strut in time to the beat, and we die a little every time we are not chosen.

But we don't have to wait long.

The taste of beer makes everything seem brighter.

It's possible to settle for someone who likes the wrong bands, provided they posture with confidence and drunken finesse.

The stench of beer sicked up and stagnating in sinks in the women's bathroom is unappetising. It makes us gag. But we suppress the urge to vomit when the winners stick their long tongues into our mouths, hungry for more than just worms.

And that's how easy it is.

As we leave the hall, arms linked through skinny wing-bones, we notice the ostrich hitting on a bird in patched jeans with broken feathers in her hair, and we know we are all the same. All hunters in an artificial paradise, waiting for something we can't name.

Discarded Fruit

Mangoes are my favourite fruit. They haven't always been. I once thought I could kill for lychees. Strawberries advertise their joy in red-stained seduction, but reality does not match their promise.

The strangeness of paw paws appeals when I'm in the mood for something antagonistic.

Grapes are too sugary, and persimmons shouldn't even be food. Whoever decided they were edible?

The aromatic intensity of golden kiwi fruit is an unexpected gift, neither cheapened by their abundance, nor sullied by acidity.

Bananas are an everyday friend, sharing the nobility of fresh food with the decadence of confectionery. Pears are as comfortable as a blanket, but must be consumed between hardness and rot. Indecision is your enemy with this shapely fruit.

Grapefruit are captured sunshine.

But the best fruit of all is a woman.

She is soft and sweet, yet take too much and you will suffer.

She has been ascribed a lascivious role with apples in the battle between serpent and god, but in my eyes she shares much in common with this humblest of fruit. A rich pseudo-carp flesh encases the potential for new life. She is the green of renewal. She is the crimson of desire.

The echo of a father's voice warns:

Beware of false lovers. They will suck the juice from a girl, and discard what's left in the gutter.

My father kept his apples carefully. They were preserved in the cellar, layers of newspaper between each storey of fruit to keep the light out.

Between Meals

Baby birds scatter like seed in the wind. They return to their mother between meals, hoping for optional extras, or a few coins if they need to make the rent before Monday.

"Where are we from?" they ask.

The mother pecks around for an answer and it is always the same. She will throw out a long word or two, like loose grain.

Deracination.

Fragmented history.

Loss of cultural identity.

The chicks laugh at their mother's verbosity.

"What happened to our ancestors?" they ask.

"We lost them when you were little more than eggs," she says.

The little ones preen each other's feathers with scarlet beaks. They don't miss what they never had.

This is What We Learn
at the Workplace
Part One

A galley of machines hisses and spits out answers.

This is where we work.

It is a place where we learn blood holds the answers to our history, our lives and our deaths.

There is a sucking, and a gurgling, pressure measured in increments by a mercury manometer. The click-clack-ching of a mechanical counter sings like a cash register. Blue-purple spheres stare out under microscope eyepieces, revealing the language of disease. Blasts. Toxic granulation. Haemolysis. Danger.

An indicator light blinks with cold precision. Rats' eye LEDs. Blood plasma turns, thickens, and traps a steel ball. This person's prothrombin time is within the therapeutic range. Good.

So many secrets, so much to learn. Every time we discover something new, it's like reaching the top of a mountain. We can see the next peak, but we're eager to scale its heights.

The Thickening of Blood

It begins when you are a child, in the pre-antibiotic dawn of an Indian summer, one of six siblings, five of whom will eventually die of broken heart valves or diabetes.

But let us say for now, you are a child, a child who loves to dance, to play in the gardens in Jalpaiguri, pulling fruit from trees, making up names for birds and insects. You dance to the tune of rain hammering the metal roof of your grandparents' home.

Schoolboys tease you for the way you pull your embroidery thread, the way you draw your arm out *so* far. You grow into a young woman who learns to sing *Rabindra Sangeet.* You attend university, so rare for a girl at the time.

When you marry my father, it is your B.A. he sees, though he is not blind to your beauty. His parents have promised him to someone else. But he chooses you. He is unaware that a childhood infection has marked you and left you damaged.

When my siblings and I are born, the births are difficult, but you survive. My sister and I are ripped out, my brother extricated by Caesarean section. His birth leaves a ladder of scars on your body. Later, the surgeon who replaces your faulty heart valve will add to the pattern.

You are prescribed warfarin and we joke about rat poison. You have never liked rodents. The brown pills have a line scored through the centre. Sometimes you break them in half, but I do not understand why. "It's to thin my blood," you say, though that does not explain why sometimes you take two, sometimes two and a half.

The blood moves thickly through your veins, though not as thickly as before.

The cartoon image in my mind helps me make sense of it. Your blood is like warmed syrup, or a milkier porridge.

When I leave home, I am less enthusiastic than you were about gaining an education, perhaps because the motivation comes from my father, not me. But I graduate regardless. My father is not an easy man to disobey.

I learn about physiology. I learn about pharmacology. I learn about blood. I learn that the thickness of blood depends on many factors. I learn why this is important for people like you, whose blood eddies and stagnates in places it should not.

Through the years, the art of hematology lures me down its blood-lined path.

I show you vials of blood in the laboratory where I work. Red fluid sucked through tubes, rotated in centrifuges, curdled with chemicals. You watch a steel ball become enmeshed in the apparatus, and appear to understand my explanation.

"It's to see how readily a person's blood clots," I tell you, conscious of your sari sweeping the detritus on the laboratory floor. I search for words to explain how warfarin changes things. You watch the indicator lights on the analyser. Red LEDs like rats' eyes.

The blood plasma turns thickly, and traps the steel ball.

Two tablets, sometimes two and a half.

Later we share a meal before you return to my father. I have become accustomed to his stony silences. He is not an easy man to please. He will not visit the laboratory.

"If only you had done something to make him proud," you say, "not just a lab technician." I flinch at the relegation of my status as a scientist, but I don't correct you. I absorb the criticism, as if the responsibility for my father's judgment is mine alone.

A wall forms between us like a hardened artery. It is fifty feet high. We rarely speak. I forget to ask about your warfarin, and you choose not to ask me about anything.

When my daughter is born, she is the catalyst that severs our ties for good. She is the glue that links me to my partner, the one you could not eradicate. I measure a person's worth using different parameters. But how would I know what's right?

Your blood flows like setting concrete through your circulation.

Blood is no thicker than water, and yet it sets like yoghurt between us.

My daughter has just turned eleven when you are admitted to hospital in India. Life has changed since you returned to your country of birth. Some things are better, others worse, but medical care in a semi-rural paradise is at the whim of the gods.

My eleven-year-old looks out of the aircraft as we land. Green. Yellow. Brown. She is engulfed by warm smells. The sounds of street sellers. The desperation of traffic. The howl of pariah dogs. The pathos of street urchins.

My father drives to the hospital in silence. You are conscious, but uncomfortable. One side of your face droops like melted plastic. You semi-smile at my child, though your eye-patch frightens her. The visit is painful for all of us.

"She's bled into the base of her brain," I tell my sister over the crackling international phone line. "It's like a stroke. She's lost power on one side of her face." I wonder as I speak, whether it means you will have to learn to turn the other cheek in arguments.

"Her warfarin?" my sister asks, so I tell her you took too much.

My father and I visit you every day. He has few words, but confides his anxieties. We almost connect. We are almost like father and daughter ought to be. My confidence increases, and I venture deeper into the morass of confusion surrounding your overdosing. I ask how often you have your blood tests done. I ask about the laboratories you visit. The answers disturb me.

"She's not been tested for some time," he says.

I ask why.

"The clinics near us," he continues, "they're not good. The roads are really bad, too. She checks her blood herself."

"How?" I ask.

"When she pricks her finger for her blood sugar."

The answer leaps into my mind before he speaks again.

The blood pumps through my brain. It gushes through my inner ear. My cheeks redden with realisation.

"When her blood looks a little thin," my father says, "your mother cuts down on her warfarin."

I am sinking.

"If it runs thick," he continues, "she takes a little more."

I showed you. I showed you how we test for warfarin.

But how would I know what's right?

When you are well enough to travel, you leave India and come to us. Further tests reveal a tumour the size of a tangerine in your head. Fragile. Prone to bleeding, should your anti-coagulation go out of control.

Your neurosurgery is scheduled for early April. Your blood flows thickly through your veins. The surgeon cuts you behind your ear. Your blood flows thickly back again.

Tense and silent as mice, we pace in the relatives' room. The surgery was long and complicated, but you have come through relatively unscathed. We thank the surgeon, the hero of the hour.

The next day, you bleed into your brain.

Within twenty-four hours you are brain dead. The coroner records your death as being caused by inappropriate treatment. You were given heparin within hours of surgery, and there are questions about whether the drug was given too soon.

I cannot hear anymore, as they determine what should have been done. I listen to the spaces between their words. I listen, hoping to hear your voice. But all I hear is silence.

This is What We Learn
at the Workplace
Part Two

So many secrets, so much to learn. Every time I discover something new, it's like reaching the top of a mountain. I can see the next peak, but am eager to scale its heights. There is pride, but there is shame too.

"If only you had done something to make your father proud." My mother's words resonated. "Not just a lab technician." Although I had flinched at the relegation of my status as a scientist, I hadn't corrected her. No matter how hard I worked, I was labelled an idiot by my own flesh and −

I worked with blood, the life force that is in all of us. I could tell you the key wavelengths of the absorption spectra attributed to haemoglobin, the red pigment in blood. It is the red of traffic light stops and danger. It is the red of meat, undercooked and raw. It is also the red of hope and love.

Let me tell you a story about a place where I once worked.

Trainee haematology scientists all wanted to work at that place. A centre of excellence, a place of learning, it was also a place of earning. If you were "just a lab technician" back then, the salary was barely enough to survive on. A scientist didn't make big bucks at the centre of excellence, but they doubled their take home pay through additional nighttime duties.

She arrived for her interview wearing a salwar kameez made from suiting material. That was when the whispering began.

She started at the centre of excellence, and I found an ally. Someone else rostered to carry out routine duties, not deemed clever enough to perform specialised work.

Perhaps she was as dense as I was.

Perhaps she was another idiot.

Let me tell you about her life.

She came from a family with few academic aspirations. The boys were expected to achieve little, the girls even less. Her family marched in a different direction from mine.

She came from a culture where schooling was seen as a daily childcare facility, somewhere older children were sent so mother could look after the younger ones. They weren't sent if they were needed for something else.

She came from a culture where spouses were recruited from the wider family, decisions made to optimise the distribution of ancestral land they held.

She completed her education and left school with a full set of qualifications. She insisted she be allowed to look for work whilst awaiting the arrival of a husband. She applied for a mortgage and moved her family to a house large enough for all of them.

This woman was no idiot.

The chosen husband's appearance coincided with an increase in snide remarks and putdowns at the excellent place where she worked. Oh how we love to kick someone when they are down. She was hidden away to operate the routine blood analyser, to press a button, start, start, start, start, all day long.

She hid the bruises inside her salwar kameez, except for the ones on her face. That was the only time I saw her wear makeup.

In the staff room, they watched her break pieces from her sandwich and bring the morsels to her mouth, whilst they bit into theirs. When she left the room, her actions were dissected, analysed, criticised. They were such excellent scientists.

Although I flinched at how my colleagues treated one of their own, I didn't correct them. I didn't try to help.

And when someone did, one of the accused was suspended on full pay and then reinstated at a higher level.

So many secrets, so much to learn. There is pride, but there is shame too.

Overwhelming shame.

Ambition

My father is pleased when I tell him my daughter wants to be a lawyer or journalist. He looks at the photographs I have brought of my son practicing drop kicks and meeting members of the All Blacks at his rugby club. The wind has changed direction overnight and palm fronds sway in synchronised saccades on the trees in his garden.

"What does he want to study?" Father massages his knees, left and right together, as if he is playing the piano.

"He's only nine," I say. "Don't think he knows yet."

"Are they attending good schools?"

"What criteria do you use to judge how good a school is?"

And we're off again, doing battle on our ideological differences.

How can two people who are so similar, be so different? My father is one of the few people I know who is more stubborn than me. Both born in April, we are bulls pushing our Taurean foreheads together, snorting and scuffing the matted ground with our hooves. Only his horns are longer and built of sturdier stuff.

I'm only visiting for a few weeks. I don't want to fight.

But it's hard not to.

$$\clubsuit$$

Everything he's done has been driven by good intent. I've always known that. And I've always wanted to break free. I fear he may tie me here with invisible ropes.

I have to go back.

I have a family. Responsibilities.

But I won't go before I find out what makes him the way he is.

I should appreciate him. We don't come from people who lock their daughters away. Literally. I should be glad to have been held only by metaphorical locks and keys. Yet there were so many of them in our home, it was hard to burrow my way out. Although he wasn't one to trap his daughters in arranged marriages, he was a locksmith of the mind.

Our parents wanted bright futures for their children. They sent us to the best schools. They knew little of the poison that seeped from the mouths of children from good families who went there.

I veer the conversation back. My father is pleased my daughter wants to be a lawyer or journalist.

She goes to a school that turns out lawyers, addicts, architects and politicians. Alumni languish in prisons, and populate over-crowded housing estates with bellies full of children from serial lovers. The most well-known graduate saws sharks in half and soaks them in formaldehyde. His art is worth millions.

❖

I'll be satisfied if my daughter achieves her dream. But most of all, I will be pleased if she leads a happy life and doesn't destroy anyone else in the process.

The Basket

The basket, with its blue ribbon and cellophane, had me bursting with pride. Pride before others. Pride before a fall.

Fifty years later, I can still hear Miss Evanton's piano when I think about it. *All good gifts around us are sent from Heav'n above.* Jane Willis stands in the corner of the hall and pisses on the floor. Mrs. Booth rushes to help. The hot iron smell of urine mixes with ripe flavours from the flowers and fruit and home-baked cakes.

Alison Cockcroft brought eggs from her hens. Robert Plumb had eaten one of his pears. Dark juice stained the paper bag chocolate brown. It slumped on stage next to my basket. My wonderful basket.

Everyone looked at that basket, and my heart swelled with the honour of it.

How could she *have a basket like that?*

Well I could. Though Mother couldn't put every imaginable fruit in it — there were no mangoes, no paw paw, lychees, no guava — she'd done her best with apples from our tree, bananas from Newman's, brown with spots, and a couple of oranges I knew she'd been saving for my little brother.

How did you *get that?* Lorna Sanders hissed. Her elbow dug into my flank like a penknife into butter.

My Mum bought it, I lied.

Oh Yeah? Lorna challenged. Miss Evanton looked at us over her glasses, whilst playing *All things Bright and Beautiful.* Mrs. Booth came back with Jane Willis.

It's the best basket here, I whispered. Pride before a fall.

Yeah, but how could she afford *it?* Lorna flicked a lock of hair back with her thumb.

Oh we're not that *poor*, I said.

Christine Tennant shuffled and smoothed her hands down the front of her grey tunic. *But you haven't even got the new school uniform.* My cheeks burned with shame. I wasn't the *only* one still wearing the old navy-blue tunic, with its buttoned belt. But that didn't matter. I tried to think of something clever to say, but Mrs. Booth wagged her finger at us.

The Tall Trees in the Greenwood, I sang and focussed on my beautiful basket.

Ho-ow Great is God A-al-mi-igh-ty.

Lorna's voice swelled beside me.

Miss Gentry, the head mistress, took to the wooden podium.

Thank you Miss Evanton, she said, and bent her head.

Most gracious God, she began.

Christine sniggered beside me, and whispered to Isobel Price.

I couldn't take my eyes off the ribbon on my basket. How carefully my mother had unpinned it when the cellophane-wrapped package had arrived.

I'll put this somewhere safe, she'd said, rolling the blue satin. *We could use it again.*

We'd feasted on pineapple, tangerines, pears and grapes, green and red, seedless and plump. My mouth watered as I remembered the flavour and the exotic wildness of mangoes.

World without end, Miss Gentry continued. She told us where our harvest festival gifts would go. The man from the NSPCC would come in a van and collect them for the children. Poor Children. Orphans.

I wasn't like them. I had a mum and dad.

My mum and dad had had a restaurant. The best restaurant in town. Indian, Chinese and European cuisine. Three chefs. The fanfare of an opening ceremony. Beauty queens and cigars. Salmon vol au vents. Me boasting to anyone who'd listen about the glass dance floor, and the bar stools you could twist around on. Bouquets of flowers and the basket of fruit from the mayor.

Miss Gentry stubbed her toe on a pumpkin, orangey-green and as large as Christine Tennant's head.

Mrs. Booth had come to our restaurant once, just before it closed. I'd been too shy to say hello. Dad scolded me afterwards.

Wasn't that a teacher from your school? Why didn't you talk to her? We can't afford to lose customers.

The children started to walk out of the hall in single file. Harvest festival was over.

Within two years of opening, Mum and Dad's restaurant was over. Pride before a fall. It was in the papers. Everyone knew. People giggled and pointed. Mum caught me crying at night. When it came to harvest festival, she knew I couldn't take a tin of pineapple or bag of apples. Mum put the basket together.

That harvest festival, just for a day, I wasn't someone to be laughed at. That day, I was the girl with the best basket, and no one could ever take that away from me.

Talking too Much

The conversation thickens the air. My father and I have been talking about Mountbatten, the last Viceroy of India. I cannot tell whether he admires the man, or despises him.

The electricity is out again tonight, and the candles flicker, because there is a crack in one of the windowpanes and the crazed wind forces its way through, billowing the net curtains my long-dead mother chose years ago at Debenhams in Leicester.

"But," I interrupt, and he silences me with a phrase that makes me feel perpetually stupid.

"It's too complicated for you to understand."

"But can you *try* to explain it to me? I *want* to understand."

"Why don't you get a book out of the library and read about it?" He's animated, and the candles highlight a flickering in his eyes that show me he's getting annoyed.

"But I want to know about Partition from *your* perspective."

He tells me something about Nehru and the halving of the provinces of Punjab and Bengal. He could be reading it out of a book from the library.

I want to know about what it was like for him and his brothers and sisters. I want to know about how his parents coped with the uncertainty. I want to understand what drove my father to become the man who loved us with the fierceness of any other parent, but who was willing to fragment his family when things didn't meet with his expectations.

And what were those things?

My sister marrying a Muslim man was not what upset him, my mother had once explained. It was the calibre of said Muslim man, she reasoned.

"We had plenty of Muslim friends," my mother had said, with her habit of using the pluperfect inappropriately. "We had not been prejudiced."

"Well what then?" I'd asked.

It was hard to defend the man whom I lost respect for when my sister and he separated, but I persevered.

"If he had been a barrister, or a lawyer, or a politician," she'd continued, "then no one would have cared that he was Muslim." She'd spoken her truths as if they were self-evident. "That is what your father wanted."

I'd wanted to shake her.

"But he *was* a politician," I'd whined.

I suppose a councillor in local government wasn't up there with Nehru or Mountbatten.

My father is talking about Jinnah's policies. I realise I have zoned out and not taken in anything he is saying. Perhaps I am perpetually stupid.

I want to change the subject, so I excuse myself and visit the bathroom. I hope my cousin has left cigarettes somewhere in the room, but find none with my dull torchlight.

78

When I return, I ask about old Uncle Jack Walker, one of their first friends in Leicestershire.

We move on to discussing my mother's family.

"Your grandfather on that side owned substantial tracts of land in the Siliguri district," he says, rolling his towel into a sausage shape and tucking it behind his neck. "The area had been occupied illegally, and has now been lost from the family."

"Go on."

"The new 'owners' grow pineapples."

The power returns with a hum. The lights flicker on and the conversation drifts to fish farming, and from that to the tropical fish we kept back in England, when I was a child.

"Do you remember the catfish that used to suck the algae from the side of the tank?" I ask.

"And the fighting fish," he says. "They were beautiful."

"Yes, and those stripey ones we got that ate the other fish." I shudder at the memory of loose eyeballs hanging on a string before being snapped up by the predatory convict fish.

"Perhaps we should have carried out a mini Partition in our fish tank," my father says, with the wisdom of a politician. Too little. Too late.

And before we can outfish one another with our recollections my father tells me he has talked too much, and needs to go to bed.

Heaven Street

I can hear Uncle Jack coming.

The *tang tang tang* of his cane on the pavement says he's almost here. When the tapping stops I run to the door to let him in. Jill tugs on her lead and then follows Jack into our house.

He's brought delphiniums for Mother, and there are cigarettes in a tin for Father. We start making demands as soon as he hangs his hat on the peg. He's not even started his cup of tea.

"Sing us the *Mock Turtle's song*," I shout, pulling the sleeve of his tweed jacket. It smells of pipe and the dogginess of Jill. Mother puts a plate of custard creams out, and sips on her tea.

"A war story. Tell us about fighting the Germans." My brother makes the *phaewww-rat-a-tat* sound of gunfire, showering me with spittle and excitement.

"Ringa-ringa-roses," my sister yells. She pulls at Uncle Jack's arm, and rubs her nose onto it. She leads him to the circle of pink flowers at the centre of the rug, where we all hold hands and sing. We turn slowly until it is time to fall over. Uncle Jack rolls on the floor with the rest of us, even though he is a very old man. He laughs like a car horn, a honking sort of noise that makes me giggle.

◆

Uncle Jack makes everybody happy. He sings, plays cards and tells stories. He folds paper hats from yesterday's *Echo*, creases the pages so they flutter like sails. My brother stands tall and straight with a broom over his shoulder. He tells us it is his bayonet.

"Watch me march," he says, "I'm going to be a soldier like you."

"War's not a game," Uncle Jack says, and my brother's face collapses into a frown.

"But," the boy continues, until Father signs *hush* with his finger, and he doesn't say anything more.

After Uncle Jack leaves, I talk to my father about the war.

"Do you wish you'd been old enough to fight the Germans?" He was only a boy when the war started.

"It's hard to say," he replies, and I don't know what he means. In my mind's eye the Germans are solemn, dangerous men.

That night I dream about parachute landings and bombs.

The day Mother tells us about Uncle Jack starts like any other. It is sunny, and there are thousands of birds tweeting in the garden. She sits the three of us on the brown sofa and says, "I have some bad news." The lines on her face say more than her words.

"Is it about the war? Are we at war again?" my brother asks. His lips are stretched like elastic bands across his teeth. I wonder if he desperately wants the answer to be *yes*.

"No," Mother says. "It's nothing like that."

"What is it?" I ask. I'm a little frightened.

"This might make you sad," she says, "but Uncle Jack died yesterday."

"Was he shot by Germans?" my brother asks.

"He died of old age," Mother says.

My sister leaps up and winds around our mother's legs like a cat. "When will he come to see us?" she asks.

"He won't." Mother cups my sister's hand in hers. "When people die, they're gone for ever."

That night Uncle Jack's ghost visits me. His medals are pinned to his tweed jacket.

"What's heaven like?" I ask.

He smiles and nods, but says nothing.

"Are there Germans in heaven too?" I ask.

"Yes," he says.

"Do they wear medals too?" I ask. But Jack can't hear me. He's vanishing down the Heaven Street, with Jill a shadow behind him.

Two Gross Packages

Fireflies flicker like fragments of a silent electrical storm tonight.

Annapurna shuffles into the room, the hem of her sari sweeping the floor. She places three candles in different places, but they do little to cancel out the darkness that falls like a curtain. So fast. So complete.

The only sound between our words is air whistling through unseen crevices. Though it was stagnant and humid in the afternoon, the movement reminds me that the season for reversing winds and madness is here.

My father dismisses Annapurna, says she can leave for the night. We have military matters on our minds. We've watched a documentary on television before load shedding disrupted the power supply. It's prompted us to talk about the Second World War. My father has promised to tell me all he can remember from that era, but we arrive at it stepping backwards through a series of detours.

"Did I ever tell you about the time I applied for an export licence to move goods between Hindustan and Pakistan?" he asks.

"No." I reply.

"I did it on the advice of an uncle." He sips from a tall glass of lemon water and clears his throat. "I was young at the time. I didn't understand why he was persuading me to get involved."

"So you didn't know what the implications were?"

"Not fully," he says, "but soon a piece of paper arrived."

The piece of paper was a certificate that allowed him to sell things.

My father's words are like gouts of precious water rushing away from me. If I don't capture them now, I don't know when I'll have the opportunity to drink from this well again.

Today his enthusiasm to tell this story is spurred on by my determination to write it down.

He speaks.

I write.

When my mother was alive, she used to say, "Someone should write a book about your father. His life has been so interesting."

And although someone once wrote a thesis outlining part of her family tree, no one has ever written a book about my father's travails.

Perhaps he feels this is as near as he will come to preserving the actions and endeavours he holds dear for future generations.

He speaks slowly and clearly.

"I was still a young boy when my father, your grandfather, responded to the building tension in the lead up to Partition."

My grandfather's name was Shitul. My father tells me Shitul relocated the family from a place called Bhanga, which is located in what is now Bangladesh. They moved to what used to be Calcutta, but is now known as Kolkata. He's always pronounced it that way, though.

It was 1938, just before the rumblings of World War II ripped into the country.

My pen scratches paper in the poor light. So absorbed am I in transcribing family history, I forget to press him about how the war affected him. I forget to ask about what I'd wanted to know.

My father would have been a ten-year-old boy. It is heartening to hear him speak in such a dispassionate way. What he saw through frightened eyes is translated into a series of objective statements, as if seeing so much war and terror diluted its impact on him.

"Many families like us moved from the city when war began," he tells me, draining his glass. "They feared being bombed by the Japanese."

A moth circles the flame, singes its wings and dies a horrible death, adding the flavour of despair to my father's dry words.

"Many families moved in the opposite direction," he continues. "It was a lottery as to who went where. Whether people survived or not was a random event."

He talks without pause, jumping between childhood events and his young adult years, and back again.

"After I left school, one of my uncles persuaded me to work in a telegraph office," he says. "I'll never forget the codes we used." He tells me the training fees were high, but it was seen as a good way to eventually score a much sought after position in the Railways.

"But I knew I had more in me. I'd tap out those keys day after day, and dream of better things." He wanted to do more. That's when he applied for an export licence, as suggested by his elderly relative.

"My first export consignment was for the raw ingredients needed for making matches," he says, as if this fact is not alarming in any way. He goes on to describe how he held several cubic metres of highly flammable materials in the family home. He delights in telling me how he sold the job lot for a good price.

After that, he says, he was involved in progressively larger transactions, which earned him up to a hundred thousand rupees each. It sounds like a lot of money for the time, and it was. He illustrates how much by telling me the family, his parents, brothers and sisters, could subsist on a rupee a day when they moved to Kolkata.

Slowly the family returned to the relative affluence they had experienced before leaving their ancestral home in Bhanga. I'm not sure if there's an element of regret when he tells me how his importing and exporting business enabled his younger brothers to complete their education. One became an engineer, a metallurgist, the other a doctor. My father had no formal education himself beyond matriculating from high school and training to be a telegraphist until he was much older.

The move to the city had been hard for the family.

"A doctor we knew invited our family to live in an apartment behind his house," he continues. "It was small, but we didn't pay much rent. The agreement was that my father would work for the man."

My grandfather had a medical licentiate qualification. It meant he could work as a doctor, even though he would have needed further study to obtain his Bachelor of Medicine.

It wasn't long after they arrived in Kolkata, my father says, that grandfather set up his pharmaceutical business.

"I remember filling the orders," he says. "Someone would shout to me, asking for two gross of something or other."

"Two gross? How much is that?" I ask.

"Two gross is two hundred and eighty-eight," he tells me.

"They didn't work in round numbers," I say.

"No, I'd go out to buy the ingredients, make up the items and package them for the hospitals." He's lost in concentration. The flickering candlelight is reflected in his eyes. "There was still a huge demand after the war. We had to fill the orders within forty-eight hours."

My focus wavers. I calculate how many forty-eight hour periods would add up to two hundred and eighty-eight, and discover it is six. I visualise six parcels of magical powders destined to treat the injured.

"Your grandmother trained as a midwife at that time," he continues. "My father faced a lot of criticism for allowing that to happen."

I want to ask how many babies she delivered, but my curiosity is stifled as he presents me with different statistics.

"She earned fifty rupees a month," he says. "I remember going with her to the cashier to request an advance from time to time."

He tells me again how his sister purchased all the sugar, rice and other basics the family needed for the day with a single rupee. I'm uncertain whether he is exaggerating.

My father's stories are dotted with numbers.

When the lights come back on, we extinguish the candles and sooty fumes float into the air. Rain batters the windows.

I gather up my papers and hover around his bookcase looking for something to read before I go to sleep. Half a dozen books spill out when I try to extricate one, and land on the floor. Amongst them, a book on Einstein, a William Goldman novel and something with a bejewelled woman on the front cover. My father appears next to me. He picks the books up, puffing with the effort of bending so low.

"Sorry," I say. "I'm still as clumsy as I always was."

"Did you see this?" he asks. But before I can tell what he's pointing to, the lights go out again.

"Stupid power company," he says. We mount the spiral staircase by torchlight, heading for our bedrooms. "Remind me to show you tomorrow morning."

"Show me what?

"The book. Your uncle's book," he says.

"Which uncle?"

"My youngest brother," he says. He is referring to the metallurgist.

"He wrote a book. It's something he always wanted to do." My father stands outside his bedroom, pointing his torch towards my door.

"Yes, I'd heard he was a good all rounder."

"He was a dreamer. A bohemian."

"Before or after he left India?"

"Both. He could win anyone over. He was charming. But I'll tell you more about him later. It's time to sleep." The wind howls a little tune.

He disappears into his room. Two fireflies flicker above the doorframe he's just walked through, and I wonder whether insects dream too. Just like us.

Bearwood

The enigma that was Florence Fagan inhabited my dreams beyond the confines of the woman's life. Her gelatinous feet oozed out of patent-leather shoes like wicked butter and left their mark in the same way.

A flounce of chiffon, an ounce of perfume. The ungodly scent of rosebuds. Framed pictures of the Royal Family. Florence names her Loyal Family, one by one. My family. There's Bachu and David (whose real name she cannot articulate). She reserves the softest space in her heart for the prize-winning metallurgist who is her hero. He wears an Errol Flynn cowlick, and marries a princess from the *philosophia perennis* dynasty.

Florence is the powder-pink landlady, who bakes cake on birthdays and anniversaries. The smell of custard fills her capacious house, which stands like a palace in the heart of Bearwood. She has a ceramic atomiser with a rubber bulb. I want to squeeze that bulb even more than I want to slide down the bannisters. I pull daisy heads in her fairy garden. An uncle with metronome eyes tells me there is a horse buried in the back. The garden is peppered with stakes topped with tennis balls that Florence has painted blue. They hold the 1967 flowers up.

Florence keeps an envelope within an envelope. It contains the milk teeth of her stepchildren. She soaks her dentures in sherry.

David burns incense and builds a memorial when Florence passes. She goes like a stone from a kidney. Painful, but with the end in sight.

My Father's Medicine
Part One

My father takes his medicine like a good boy, without the need for sugar. The yellow and cerise pills for his heart and mind are sweet enough on their own.

He slips energy drops under his tongue, confident in his self-administration. He is safe in the knowledge they will make him better.

My grandmother would dispense pills and powders made by her husband to her sons and daughters when my father was a young man. He took them wordlessly, grateful, whilst he balanced the weight of family members on slender shoulders.

My father keeps a brown unguent that smells of fish by the bedroom sink. He dilutes it with a silvery spoon. When my coughing is strident and continuous, my mother coaxes me to drink the liquid, but only when the hacking is fierce enough to strip bark off trees. The medicine tastes like rotten bones, but I delight in its poisonous touch.

My brother spills the fish medicine when he tries to steal it. He makes a mess on the floor and is spanked for it. But that disaster is far less than the chaos he creates later when he sinks his fingers into cold cream and smears our mother's vermillion powder into creases and cracks in the bedroom. Everything is mixed up. He cries and cries for help. I mop up what I can and slap him for good measure. I place everything back in the drawer he pulled them from. My parents keep a tin full of pennies in there. I help myself when no one is looking.

Later, I dilute Mercurochrome in a glass, watch it change colour when the light hits it at different angles. A slice of green one moment, and a red blood window the next.

Later still, my brother and I compare notes on which of our father's pills we should steal. It turns out I have made the wiser choice, with benzos and sleeping pills. My brother took a chance with pills for high blood pressure. I tell him he could have gone blind, and slap him for good measure.

My father doesn't notice what we have taken even when I up my dose to two, four, eight times the recommended amount. He has so many pills, it's hard for him to keep track.

He's taken his medicines for so long, it is unlikely he can remember what he is trying to get better from.

The Bejewelled Woman
on the Cover

"Which uncle?" I'd asked.

"The youngest one," my father had said. He was referring to the metallurgist.

My father has been telling me our family history; stories that have echoed through generations but passed me by, because I have been living in an alternative reality.

I have been in the Land of The Ostracised for many years, but have been granted a visa that has allowed me to enter the Land of Acceptance.

"My brother wrote a book," my father had said. "It's something he always wanted to do."

I wanted to know more, but that was all that my father told me that night.

Vertical lines of rain plummet from the sky. I want to know more about the book, but the rhythm of the weather wipes out my ability to think clearly this morning. The insanity of the monsoon shouldn't last this long. I hope for clarity, but this maddening wind has taken its toll.

Perhaps it is only jetlag.

"He was a dreamer. A bohemian," my father had told me before we retired for the night. I went to bed hungry for more details.

I know little about my uncle's youth. I know even less of what he has become in recent years. I know the man in-between, a different man from the one talked about in hushed whispers in the latter years, the metallurgist who forged a double life.

To me, my uncle was the family stalwart, an anchor, the linchpin. He was the adult I wanted to become. I wanted to comprehend who he had been as a young man, perhaps to better understand the man he became later.

I met my uncle when I was five years old. He visited us with my aunt. It was a magical time. We had the tallest Christmas tree that year, the brightest lights, the whitest icing on Mother's fruitcake. The house thrummed to the rhythm of visitors who came to gaze at the star-lit couple: my uncle, who had won a gold medal at university, and his wife, who had walked hand-in-hand with every revered person in recent Indian history. They were bright. They were beautiful. They illuminated my mother and father. Their charisma diffused into all of us.

Over the years, we looked forward to their visits.

My uncle would launch into conversations everywhere we went. He said *Good Day* to shop assistants, asked them what they liked best about their work, whether they were content where they lived.

He charmed silent aunts into sharing a piece of their lives. He was equally at ease talking to politicians, musicians, actresses and other people who pretended to be something they were not.

I have the opportunity to complete the gaps and press my father for answers. He starts from the very beginning.

"I hadn't realised my mother was expecting another child," he says, while rain beats the ground to mud.

"How could you not have known?" I ask.

"I was quite naive about that sort of thing." It's unusual for my father to be so frank. "The first I knew about it was when a searing cry rang through the house." He settles back in his chair to enjoy his yarn. "Someone told me I had a new brother."

He tells me a few anecdotes about when they were young. He talks of splashing around in swimming holes. He tells me how they used to capture lizards, repulsed when they shed their writhing tails. Then he skips to describing my uncle as a young man.

"He had great aspirations to become a poet. Like Tagore, or the European Romantics."

My uncle had kept long flowing locks, dressed with artistic flair. He went reluctantly to his interview at engineering college, as directed by my grandfather. Afterwards, one of the professors was heard to remark, *Has that young man come here to perform theatre?*

Although that college accepted him, my uncle studied half-heartedly. My father discovered partway through the year that he had been bunking off classes, and eventually been expelled for non-payment of fees. My father paid off the arrears and had his younger brother re-admitted.

Later, my father discovered his brother had been helping out one of their relatives who had been short of cash. That's where his college fees had gone. My uncle had returned to his classes with renewed enthusiasm, and became an excellent student.

That's how the story goes.

Next, my father talks about my uncle's dark years; the straying from his wife and sons, the wild dreams, the over-ambitious schemes.

"Through all that despair," my father says, "your uncle managed to write this book."

He hands me a tome with a dusky woman on the cover. She wears a jewel on her forehead.

"I'd love to read it," I say.

"Keep it," my father says. "I have several copies. And there's another manuscript somewhere, an unpublished sequel."

I don't sleep much that night, as I'm drawn into the world my uncle has created on paper. It is a world I didn't know he inhabited. His characters are stuck on a cyclic journey, chasing dreams of wealth and good fortune.

I'm uncertain whether his story is told with irony or not.

You learn something of the creator through the actions of the created.

I wish that I hadn't, and prefer instead to remember the tallest Christmas trees, the brightest stars.

❖

The next day, I try to return the book, but my father insists I take it with me when I leave. It's still raining.

I haven't seen my uncle for years. But I'm surprised we never bumped into each other on the highways and low lanes in The Land of the Ostracised, when we both lived there.

Perhaps we'll meet again in a different land. If we do, I'll ask what he wrote in the sequel. And because he's no longer with us, and because this is a place of dreams, I'll ask him to write another book. One just for me. One that shows how an uncle can ignite a five-year-old child with harmony and magic. One that will help me remember my uncle as he was when I first met him.

Scissor Cuts

When your mother dies, it haunts like scissor cuts against the grain of your thinking.

It doesn't matter that you weren't close. It doesn't matter that you didn't see her often. It doesn't matter that you can't forget the awful things she said.

You remember the small things that were huge.

You remember the fruit basket she made for school, how she snipped blue ribbon and tied it just so to hold the cellophane in place over globular fruit and glabrous nuts.

You remember how she tried to teach you to knit. How you both nearly died laughing when the teddy bear scarf grew from thirty-two to seventy-two stiches wide.

You remember how she showed you and your sister pictures of a baby growing in a mummy's tummy before the new brother came. You remember accepting her lies about how he got there, because you didn't know any better, and because sometimes there is virtue in the lies people tell.

You remember her parting mounds of flour with a metal spoon to make a well, though she couldn't pronounce the word "well" correctly. She cracked an egg and you watched it slip into the "vell". You'd lick the spoon later. The mixture always tasted better than the cake.

You remember how she said you'd get married when you grew up, and that you wouldn't be scared, how she laughed when you screamed that you never would.

You remember her tying a chef's apron around her loose belly and cooking for hours when the Chinese cook was ill while you overdosed on glacé cherries.

You remember gliding over the sea in a ship on holiday, feeling like you were a woman though you were still a child, because she let you use her turquoise eyeshadow.

You remember the matryoshka dolls she bought in Poreč, generation swallowed by generation.

You remember that like the children who come after you, you and your mother are different, yet you are the same.

Harborne High Street

My mother's blood types as B positive, and she lives up to her group. I rub her shoulders ever so gently. I am scared of breaking her fragile body.

I don't want to leave you, I say. I try not to make my voice small, like a child's.

Be positive. She smiles as she says it. I hesitate at her bedside. *I'll be up and about before you know it.* Her movements are slow and mechanical after surgery. Her hair is matted around the incision point. The bag of fluid on a stand refracts window-light like a jewel.

There's no need to stay. Go back home — your work — your children. Be careful on the road.

She holds my hands in her bruised ones. My mother sees major danger on minor roads. I fail to see the arteriole in her head that throbs with the excitement of blood. She warns me, her eyes chameleon-like with concern: *It's dangerous out there. There's sleet and the rain. Drive carefully.*

I tell her to recover quickly, as if she can will the body parts to knit together faster by thinking about it.

We have a plan, I say. *Remember you asked me to take you to the second-hand shops on Harborne High Street?*

I don't look back when I leave. I never do. I don't know if she is smiling or not. Alcohol hand-cleanser, sharp as gin, evaporates without comment.

I plan my next visit to the rhythm of windscreen wipers. Somewhere between an overdue report and next Tuesday, I'll come again.

I'm putting my youngest to bed when the phone rings. Mother has bled into her brain. She is not expected to live. A thought reverberates as I fill the dishwasher. *The second-hand shops on Harborne High Street.* It was the last thing I said to her. My fingers knit around the cutlery like hungry snakes. A plate slips and breaks in two. Something nags from within. I should be by her side, but there's nothing I can do. There's rain in the air, wine in my veins. I don't rush back to her ventilated body that night. There's little point. The blood has already done its damage, her less than positive blood. *Tomorrow*, I whisper to myself.

The hospital tang hits me like an over-ripe blanket. I meet the others in the relatives' room. We approach her bedside, a ring of semi-orphaned siblings. I touch the shadow of a tear that seeps from her unseeing eye, and place a second-hand book from Harborne High Street on her bedside.

Haunted by Dream Fathers

He says, "I may not be here much longer."

Before this, we were remembering my mother's final days. When he talks about leaving, I know my father isn't discussing remaining in the villa or the city or even whether he plans to stay in the monsoon-drenched country for the foreseeable future.

He has warned us of his imminent death for years.

When I was a child, my father left the house at night to work evening shifts, or to supply groceries to the restaurants in the vicinity. My mother worried he would work himself into an early grave.

I found it hard to sleep, tormented by death demons.

You'll be left fatherless. Motherless. You'll be taken into care. Separated from your brother and sister.

His hands, covered in corrugated skin, shake as he turns a paperback book over and over, warping the pages. Father is well into his seventies. The opportunity for an early and glorious death has passed him by.

The words of long-gone schoolteachers echo through the corridor of my mind.

Domesticated cats live for twelve to fifteen years, fewer in the wild.

Mice four.

Galápagos tortoises almost two hundred.

The expected human lifespan is three score and ten years.

I disconnect the emotions thumping through my chest. One of the things I admire most in my father is his ability to stick to facts, his contempt for euphemisms, his plain speaking.

"Is it the process of dying you fear," I ask, "or the thought of not being around anymore?"

"It's the idea of not being here," he says. "The thought of the world still going on without me." He puts the book down. A bejewelled woman stares from the front cover.

I uncross my arms. "Isn't that good in a way?"

"What do you mean?" His eyes are firefly bright. The heaviness of the *W* in *what* is curdled milk at the back of his throat.

"Perhaps neither of us will be here to witness the unnecessary destruction of the earth."

My father stiffens. He has always viewed my concerns about the environment as an indulgence. "There are better things to worry about than a few birds and elephants dying here and there," he says. "The world will still be here. I won't."

"But really," I push. "What are you most frightened about? We're all going to die. What is it you find least acceptable?"

"It's not the inevitability of dying. If I could die in peace, I'd rest easily at night if — "

"Is it the thought of pain?" I persevere, even though his shoulders stiffen with unease.

"It's the lack of control."

"There are drugs," I continue. "Ways to make the end easier to bear."

"No," he says, worrying the pages of the book through his fingers. In all the days I've been here, I haven't seen him read a single page. "No. You don't have any idea."

"Then tell me."

His greatest fear: He believes someone, dacoits he calls them, will scale the high walls and enter the compound. He believes he will be taken away and held captive. My father tells me this with the calm rationality he uses when talking about local government, cataracts, or the cost of rice.

There is nothing I can say to alleviate his fears about being tortured by unknown hands. It has happened, he assures me, to people who live in the district. It's happened many times.

There is nothing I can do to prevent his death demons from tormenting him.

Later I dream of fictional fathers. Some are like him. Others are not. Some are kind. Some are distant. In my dreams, they have different names: Sunil, Tony, Horen, Coco, Mukanda. Some are light-hearted and funny. Others try their whole lives to escape the shadows that define them.

Shadow

Some shadows are forgotten moments that stick to a soul.

One of eight children, Mukunda was destined to outlive his siblings. Two brothers died before he was born. Pneumonia visited Ashok, took him for a walk and never came back. The shadow drew breath. Tuberculosis came dancing, rattling the chests of all it touched, spraying the walls red. It took Khoka by the hand, and left with him.

Mukunda was only three when Dysentery gushed through the village, inviting the children to play. With asafoetida breath, the disease nearly took the boy with it, but waltzed away empty-handed.

Mukunda lived with the shadowy figure on his shoulder, a portent to remind him of the impermanence of life. It followed him through vibrant summers. The darkness was there when monsoon rains washed away the mud-shacks where he lived, taking baby Deepa with it. It followed Mukunda wherever he went.

I see everything you do, the misty shape whispered in his ear. *I count all your dues.*

The shadow followed him into adulthood. His sister Priyah died in childbirth, and his younger brother Tarun slipped under the wheels of a truck whilst taking his father's tiffin carrier to work.

The ghostly form kissed Mukunda's children on the forehead as they came into the world. Their squawking, defecating bodies turned blue when the shadow passed through them.

As Mukunda lay drifting to sleep, sometimes he'd think the figure had left. The relief almost made him cry. Then he'd turn over, see dark triangles pecking his wife's face, and the comfort would wash away like rain.

The shape might present as a raven, or a coal-black monkey, hanging by its tail from the sacred figs in the jungle. Mukunda told himself the shadow was part of his imagination. But whenever he thought he'd escaped, its dark fingers crept back into his core.

When the youngest of his children married and left for her new home, Mukunda's brother Rustom with the rheumatic heart caught a cold and died.

The dark form pricked Mukanda's conscience.

Why are you still here? the shadow asked.

A year later, Mukanda's sister Kirti pricked a blister on her finger with a needle. Something got into her blood, and left her dead.

I'm watching you, the shadow told Mukunda.

Days come and go. Months. Years. The shadow stays. It is a punishment, a stain. It is a reminder that Mukunda has lived when the others didn't.

It is a forgotten moment that attached itself to his soul.

Super 8 Camera

He came home one day with a super 8 movie camera. When he placed the silver gadget on the table, we crowded around to get a better look. My sister pressed a button and nothing happened.

"How much will the film cost?" my mother asked. "And the developing. It's not just the price of the camera." Her face elongated with anxiety. It hadn't been that long since we'd fallen on hard times.

My father had been to an auction.

Auctions were where he acquired much of the paraphernalia that filled the windowless rooms in our wide and rambling house.

Despite her initial reticence, my mother was interested. She stroked the chrome-plated logo, peeped through the viewfinder.

"It looks good." She pointed out features here and there. "How do you make it work?"

"It needs the right batteries."

"Hai Raam! You haven't seen it working? How do you know it's not broken?" My mother flicked her husband an accusatory stare.

"I got it for a very good price," he said, as if that was the only explanation required.

❖

Although it was the first time my father had brought home a movie camera, it wasn't the first time he'd come home with unexpected purchases. Often he returned from the auction house with multiple unnecessary items. Cupboards overflowed. Objects sang out their uselessness like adverts.

Here I am. The ninth bicycle, rotting and chainless.

Thought you had enough reading lamps? You can never have too many! Here we are, with spent bulbs and burnt out plugs.

I am the inside of a piano. I look like a harp. I am tuneless and irretrievably useless.

A broken television set? Don't throw me away! Somebody, somewhere might be able to repair me.

Table leg? Useless as a bone without a dog? But my wood is beautiful. I could be made into something wonderful.

Handle-less pans. Handle-less pans. Porridge burnt onto the bottom, blackened soot bases. Someone once loved us, handle-less pans. We will be loved again.

My brother asked if Dad would film him practicing football.

My sister asked whether she could use it to make a movie. She started planning roles for each of her many friends.

My mother said we already had so many things in our lives that didn't work.

❖

That night I dreamed of making my first feature. All the friends I didn't have would have starring roles. The film would be about a lost girl who was found, then lost again.

It didn't matter that the camera wasn't working. Buttons had been pushed, and a chain of events unleashed.

It didn't matter, because the story was already beginning to unfold, because somewhere, somehow, it had already happened in real life.

The One In Which My Dream Father is a Duck

This time I dream my father is a duck. It's not a lucid dream, and it doesn't happen in R.E.M. sleep. It's the sort of dream that could redefine itself as real, and go rushing to the city on a bus.

He is a mother duck in the dream, though he remains, as always, distinctly male. There are drake feathers in his tail, narrow and curled. He has eight ducklings, and a clutch of eggs he sits on too, hard and waxy, like raw potatoes.

He quacks with an Indian accent, the dialect unknown.

The ducklings follow in a squiggly line, when he ventures away from the nest. One wanders to the side and retches in riverside weeds. My father clasps its neck delicately with quotidian precision, and brings the young bird back in line.

He refuses bread that is hurled like abuse from the sidelines. Offerings from persons unknown don't meet with his Bengali sensibilities. He sees it as akin to begging.

Later, he splits portions of dahl bhat between the youngsters, spices his own with chilli.

When dusk falls, my avian father plucks the tallest duckling from the line, and teaches it to fly, fly, fly.

I am that bird.

The Girl They Left Behind

She is as fiery as the chilli peppers she adores and has a mind of steel. My sister is fun. She is powerful. She is someone you never want to cross.

We didn't meet until she was six and I was three. Everything was the wrong way round, inside out. We were marinated in the sound of people telling us how to be. She was told to smile. I was primed to recite lines about sharing our mother.

Everything about us was different. I'd been indulged; she had not. She was athletic; I was contemplative. I was curly; she was beautiful. She was pink and I was blue. I adored cats; she shied away from animals. She knew how to count to a hundred in Bengali; I knew the two of us had rocky times ahead.

Our father had sailed to Southampton on a ship with portholes, filled with wild stories. He planned to forge a new life in England. He left behind a wife and baby daughter. They were to follow later, but a jigsaw puzzle of family interactions meant my mother joined my father sooner than planned.

She left my sister with her mother-in-law for a few months.

Months turned to years.

❖

Years later, I ask my father what made them leave my sister behind. My questions are kind. I want to avoid accusations, only want explanations.

I am disarmed by his honesty. For someone who has not spoken to me for several years, he is open. He talks of being swayed by other people's decisions. He talks about his mother, who would not let go of the child. He tells me he didn't know how to stand up to her. My grandmother was a formidable woman.

I think of my children back home. It breaks me to be away from them for a few weeks while I visit my father. I begin to understand my sister wasn't the only victim in the play of power that took place almost half a century earlier.

"What made you change your mind about her?" I tread on dangerous ground. My father knows I'm not talking about the first time he left my sister behind. It's something that has happened more than once, but for different reasons. "About resuming contact with her," I add, to be sure he knows. I want to understand why after being ostracised for more than a decade, he has allowed my sister and I back into his life.

"I'm finding all this reminiscing too difficult," he responds. "I need to rest." He heads for the spiral staircase that leads to his bedroom. "Tell Annapurna not to bring me any tea this afternoon."

I know then, that I have pushed him too far.

A Girl Named Prayer

It stops raining the day the Gupta family come to visit, but the demonic wind still cuts through trees, tossing cotton wool clouds into the dilute Bagaanabad sky.

I haven't seen Nakul Gupta since we were children. Now I face a middle-aged man with a weighty paunch to match my own. He is accompanied by a silent wife and moon-faced daughter. The child has a darker skin-tone than either parent.

Old "Uncle" Gupta was one of my father's oldest friends. They'd been at school together in Kolkata. They had clung to each other like moths to flypaper when both men emigrated to England in the 1950s.

Our family kept in contact with the Guptas over the years. We'd travel to the south of the country for the weekend. I'd lie in the guest bed, staring up at glass-framed photos of sombre Gupta relatives on the wall.

They had a shrine like my grandmother's, displaying images of deities I didn't recognise. The sharp features and severed head necklaces scared me. My mother told me the Guptas had a different god, yet all gods were the same. I knew it was one of those complicated adult things children weren't even supposed to understand. I was too young to know what philosophia perennis meant at the age of six. I'm not sure even now whether I understand the universal truth that is shared by all religions. It's hard for an atheist.

My siblings and I would play with Nakul and his younger brother Pushpa. I was Robin to Nakul's Batman. My sister nominated roles for each of us when we became *The Monkees*. I wanted to be Mickey Dolenz, but was usually re-cast as a manager or inexplicable chimpanzee. We'd become secret agents and disappear into the world of *The Man from U.N.C.L.E*, or turn into different incarnations of Tarzan during long hazy days in the Guptas' back yard.

The Guptas returned to India decades before my parents did.

I didn't see Nakul again until we were much older. By then, he'd progressed beyond childhood games based on British television programmes, and epitomised what it meant to be cool in 1970s Calcutta.

We found little in common.

Thirty years later, we find a shared goal. Nakul is impressed by my recent move to New Zealand. He also wants to move to a better place. He asks about the immigration process and wonders whether I can help him with an application. I tell Nakul about the skills list and refer him to an appropriate website.

I neither have the contacts nor lack of integrity to expedite the process.

Nakul takes the china teacup Annapurna offers and nods his acceptance. My father's servant averts her eyes. It isn't in her rules of etiquette to receive thanks or acknowledgement. She presses a biscuit into Nakul's daughter's palm.

Pratana is a sober child, who sits close to her mother. Nakul's wife makes a small gesture of permission, and the child bites into the *Rich Tea* biscuit. I learn they have named their adopted daughter *Pratana*, a prayer.

Nakul's parents smile with barely concealed pride as their granddaughter sweeps biscuit crumbs off her dress into a cupped hand and asks where she should tip them.

Remembering comments made by various aunts and cousins about adoption, I wonder why this family is not bound by the same prejudice.

I've heard his sons and daughters aren't his real *children.*

They're different. They are not blood.

There is nothing stronger than the tie of family. Real *family.*

I am proud of my old friend and his wife for *their* integrity. I admire their ability to ride beyond the wheels of convention in order to find the answer to their own prayers.

The prayers are answered in the form of this sweet-natured girl who looks like neither of them.

Moving to a Better Place

My father farewells my grandfather for the last time. It happens several years before I am born.

The old man slips an arm around his son's shoulder.

"I'll never see you again, shall I?"

My father doesn't say anything, because he knows the older man's words are true. My uncle, his youngest brother, has left a year or so earlier. His parents see their children spill away, all going to a better place. A place without them.

My grandfather is a shadow on the platform. His wife stands beside him swallowing silent tears.

The train screams a warning.

A ship sucks and glides through the surrounding water.

My father accepts his losses, because he wants to move to a better place.

All over the world, and throughout time, people are moving to better places. Some succeed. Some fail.

When my father reaches his destination his brother lends him his best coat. It has holes at the elbows. Two Bengalis looking out for one another. They are cold, but they are happy.

For too long now, they have dreamed of moving to a better place.

It will be a while before they feel the need to move again.

O

Behind the letter 'O', I realise my life means nothing without you.

It's not warm. Neon lights create very little heat. The 'E' flickers on and off like the start of a fit, and the 'L' lies over loose tiles. We have some protection here, when the wind isn't blowing the wrong way.

I pull the fur of your hood back and swipe your brow. Drops of rain mingle with pearls of sweat. You moan, and creak the thick plastic I have draped around your body. Your fevered voice reminds me of when you were little.

"Aak deen shob thik hoy jabay," Ma used to say when floodwaters threatened. *One day everything will be all right.*

We came to this country for a better life. We came to survive. With Ma and Baba gone, it's just you and me.

I'll visit the rubbish bins, bring hot dogs, burger buns with green spots removed. If we're lucky, cola dregs in a paper cup.

"Jol khabo," you cry for a drink. Then you lick the rain from your lips.

A man leaves the motel. The roundness of his belly strains through the whiteness of his shirt. He slams his car boot and looks up. Maybe he heard you. I push my hand over your mouth to subdue your voice. Your face is firefly hot.

"Aak deen shob thik hoy jabay," I croon.

You close your eyes little brother, and I long for you to open them again.

I cradle you in the 'V' of my arms.

The Knot in the Cream Sari

My grandmother used to tie knots in the *achhaal* of her saris. After she became a widow she only wore variations of the shade white. The knots were there to remind her she had unfinished business.

Perhaps she had left milk curds straining in a piece of muslin, or maybe she needed to bring the washing in. Sometimes the knots were to remind her she needed to make extra prayers that day. It could be the Remembrance Day for a particular god. It might be the anniversary of a significant death in the family.

Today, I'm helping my father to clear away some of the junk he has collected over the years.

"Where do we take these things?" I ask. "Is there a municipal dump near here?"

My father laughs, as if I have asked if there is a nuclear rocket launcher in his back garden. What he does have though, is an area that acts as landfill, where we are to dump out of date vials of insulin from when my mother was alive, mouldy books they shipped from England that are covered in a fine layer of mildew, and a decade's worth of paperwork, if he can be persuaded it is never likely to be useful again.

We move one box of documents and a mouse leaps onto my shoulder and then jumps onto him. My father tells me what wants saving then leaves me to sort through more piles of memories.

I have trouble remembering what he asked me to save, and what can be thrown out.

Later I call Annapurna away from kitchen duties and ask her for help in shifting piles of rubbish to the unofficial dump. A barrage of protestations hinders me: *you can't throw this out* and *we might be able to sell that.*

Perhaps this is a job for another day.

I find my father in the lounge. He's snoring lightly in his chair, and is startled by my presence.

"Sorry I woke you," I say.

"Stop doing that now," he says. "Come and sit with me. You'll leave in a few days."

We drink the tea that Annapurna brings and talk. I am aware I haven't utilised this opportunity to find out all I wanted to know about my father's past. I'll fly home in less than forty-eight hours, still grappling with our differences, still searching for common ground.

"Tell me something more about what it was like when the war broke out."

I know World War II coincides with one of the darkest periods in India's history. I know I might find some answers here.

My father tells me how they feared air raids. He talks about curfews, rations and corruption. He speaks of famine, and how it selectively wiped out certain sections of society, whilst others were left unaffected. He talks about seeing bodies in the streets, moist and swollen by putrefaction.

Once he's begun, he doesn't want to stop.

The wind picks up again and screams a warning through the shutters.

I understand a little more about my father this day, as a maddening wind threatens. I learn something about how his values were shaped. About his hopes and disappointment. But it is still not enough.

Eventually, he is too tired to talk any more. It's time for his siesta.

On resuming my search for things to discard, I find a white sari, musty and folded. One of the corners has a knot tied in it.

Perhaps it will take someone different to clear my father's house, someone stronger than I am.

Unused Currency

I count my mother's tears in reflected dollar signs on shop windows. She would have longed for a day like this.

Our mother is behind us in all our home movies. My father's memories of her are different from my own.

We travel to the market. It's cloudy, but the wind is not as wild as it has been. There are some supplies my father doesn't trust Annapurna to purchase. He wants to select the best. Make the right choices. While we are there, he takes me to a tailor, tells me to choose whatever I want. They will measure my body and make a garment overnight. Like elves do.

Father argues with stallholders, reading from a script in his head. The wind picks up. His dour expression is beaten into anger. I look the other way. The rice he buys is packed in a brown paper carton. He gives it to me to hold under my arm, just as I carry his other belongings in my handbag. Men never have enough room in their pockets for everything. Wallets. Cigarettes. Firearms.

A search through redundant memory yields silent treasure. There is the time he explained how sixpences were made. The way he would watch football with us, providing a running commentary, supporting the opposing team to give us something to fight against. Once, we swam out to a pontoon together and back again. We didn't drown. The sincerity of his smile at a cousin's wedding. How he made spaghetti and eggs when our mother was in hospital giving birth to our baby brother. How he charmed visitors with his wit and intelligence. The time he wrote *mother* in window condensation, because he hadn't seen our grandmother for a year. His kindness in picking up a stranger at the side of the road who had too many cases to carry onto the bus. The way he shared what he had, to help others lead a better life. How he lied to us and said Father Christmas was real, even though he didn't believe in fairy stories.

Sometimes there is virtue in the lies we tell.

How he slipped a sliver of cabbage he was dicing into his mouth, and told me it was a caterpillar.

I thought he would die. He did die eventually, cocooned in a sac to stop him from getting bedsores. He did die, but not then. Not from caterpillar poisoning.

The weight of my father's belongings makes my handbag swing in simple harmonic motion. I have threatened to tell anyone who looks inside that the bag belongs to him.

When we return to my father's house, Annapurna has made a special meal. She's remembered all the dishes I told her I liked. Even the ones I lied about.

It's nearly time to leave.

It's hard to lose something I have found after so long.

❖

Annapurna takes the roll of cash I tuck into her hand before I go. She doesn't smile. She doesn't meet my eye. It's the way things are done around here. The roll contains a lot of money. All of these things and more are the currency by which we are measured. My father has advised me to give her something. Not too little. Not too much.

When he asks, I lie about the amount though. Sometimes there is virtue in the lies we tell.

Kopal

During the weeks I have been visiting my father, rain has washed channels into the dirt around us. On the few dry monsoon days the wind has howled like a dog and threatened to blow madness into the minds of sane people.

He rarely mentions my dead mother. When he does, my father's eyes glaze with tears.

He thinks I don't notice.

Between us, we sabotaged the final years of her life, and sank my mother into an abyss as deep as the crypts I dream about, the underground voids where I meet the ghosts of our family.

He doesn't have long to live. This knowledge peppers all our actions, and drains the salt from our wounds. He could blame me for going against the grain. I could accuse him of churlishness for allowing him to take my mother away for so many years.

But we have reached a precarious truce.

As the wind penetrates the walls and rattles the windows, I reflect that our peace has come too late.

When my mother was alive, she spoke of her future being written on her forehead.

Ayta amar kopal.

This is my fate.

This is my fate, my ill fate, written in blood
in the shadow of a crazed wind.

Garden of Eden Park

My father discovered social networking when he was in his eighties. His quivering fingers didn't navigate the keyboard as smoothly as his grandchildren's did, but he persevered. He mastered e-mail, though he preferred to write letters with his tortoise-shell fountain pen. Ashokan lion stamps glared from powder-blue envelopes, in the cardboard box where I collected his correspondence.

My brother gave Dad a laptop when he visited him in India. I hoped he'd connect with family all over the world. It was to save him from loneliness.

"Look at my machine," he told friends. "It's from my son." They taught him to e-mail and introduced him to social media.

A flurry of Internet activity ensued. I sent photos of my children, uploaded their artwork. I made friend suggestions for relatives in Europe and America. My nephew posed in cricket whites on his grandfather's timeline. Dad chatted with aunts in America and nieces in Norway. He loved simultaneously exchanging information between Wisconsin, Oslo and Auckland.

There were jokes, links to songs and images of my mother smiling through dense foliage. Monsoon charged air wrapped me in its wet warmth, as I remembered Mum's embrace, the velvet of her cheek. I imagined she was still alive.

My brother posted a picture of Dad at the cricket at Eden Gardens in Kolkata. It was an old photo with a tea stain on the corner. Underneath, a string of comments grew. I suggested Dad should come visit. The cricket may not be as good at Eden Park, but it would be good for him. However, the frailty of old age was marking my father's bones, making travel difficult.

Dad's fingers, deformed by arthritis, found it difficult to punch computer keys. Late last year, he lost patience with his "machine", and that was the end of his cyber-experience. His accounts remain active, and people post messages on birthdays and festivals. He never reads them.

I get a warm feeling when I recall how serendipity knocked on my office door last month. My supervisor only just caught me as I left one evening.

"Can you spare a minute?"

He pulled a folder out of a drawer.

"No one else can make the Indian meeting. Can you go?"

Dad was sick. I didn't have enough leave to visit him.

"I'll go," I said without hesitation.

I flick through the in-flight magazine as we taxi along the runway. Stroking my finger over the familiar koru I find I'm too emotional to read. It's too late.

My father died two days ago.

After the meeting, my brother and I will pour Dad's ashes into the Ganges. Two Bengalis side-by-side with sandalwood tikkas on our foreheads.

At thirty-three thousand feet, I contemplate my father's experiences as a young man in the 1950s. He left India, set sail for a new life. Sailed on a sea of hope towards his home for the next twenty-seven years. My brother and I were born overseas. It was home until the family scattered again like glass beads. My parents had missed their homeland.

I imagine my father disembarking. He carries a leather case covered in stickers from previous ports of call. He locates a post office, sends a telegram home.

I visualise him finding his way. He shivers after the cocooning warmth of India. Does the fatty tang of fish and chips turn his stomach? Or is he too hungry to care? Traffic lights, Coca Cola. Are these experiences comforting or alien?

Dad reaches his destination and his brother lends him his best coat. It has holes at the elbows. Two Bengalis looking out for one another. My father works in a restaurant to finance his studies. The cost of phone calls to India is prohibitive. His parents don't own a telephone anyway. I visualise the blue paper, thin as a dragonfly's wing, on which he forms the words for his letters. His mother writes every week, though her feelings lose their intensity as the lines of Bengali script travel across the world.

Dad chats to the Pakistani waiter. The man has a wife and child back home. He has another wife, an Irish woman whom he refers to as "Bhhalarri". Valerie keeps the waiter warm on icy nights. She saves him from loneliness.

As we come in to land, vibrant squares of farmland fluoresce in yellow light. My brother will arrive soon. I check my phone while I wait. There are messages flooding onto my father's timeline. He receives messages on birthdays and festivals.

Rest in peace.

Remembering a wonderful Uncle.

Always in our minds.

He'll never read them.

My Father's Medicine Part Two

When my father died, we found a cupboard full of unused medicine.

There were tablets in blister packs, pills in capped containers, lotions in phials, and vials of potions. We discovered cartons of camphor oil, a brace of Barbary duck feathers for brackishness, prune juice in bottles for constipation. There was a battalion of homeopathic remedies to treat anything from moles to morning sickness; cures before *mol* or after *morn* were missing. We found creams and poultices, plasters and bandages, corsets and stockings. There was a sphygmomanometer, a stethoscope, and something to measure blood sugar with, though the batteries had expired and leaked. We found liquids to soften corns and gels to harden fingernails. There was enough dental floss to strangle an elephant, and doses of drugs that could *kill* an elephant and render the floss unnecessary. There were sleeping pills with childproof lids, and an embrocation for successful marriage. There were painkillers in the form of liquids, pills and suppositories. We found prescriptions for antibiotics for him under differing dates of birth, addresses old and new. We found ones for our mother dated well after she was dead and gone. We found contraceptive pills, and wonder drugs to reverse the effects of aging. There were part-used packs of cough lozenges, and balms to soothe aching limbs. We found cartons of happiness cream, and bottles of sweet temperament, cinnamon-flavoured and coated in sugar powder. There was gum for good dental hygiene and to relieve the monotony of the first Monday of the month. Hidden beneath a bale of cotton wool were Parma violets for bad breath, a packet of long-acting aspirin, and a pot of powders to combat loneliness.

And in amongst all that stuff, we didn't find a single way to get him back so he could explain to us what it was all for, seeing as he hadn't used any of it.

One Night

One night I visit you on Google Maps. The third lamppost on the right is still there, though the magnolia tree has disappeared. The garden isn't there anymore.

You appear in pre-cell-phone movies, an extra buying a newspaper in an airport. A child with golden hair in a crowd. Time passes differently in matte celluloid.

On YouTube clips of opera-writing prodigies, you clean windows, serve coffee, mow lawns. Sepia-bound, lemon-scented. In that world, you are not dead.

Swimming

You make me believe I can swim, when you carry me through the water on your back, strong as a bear, safe as a house. We glide together like a hump-backed fish. I cannot remember being cold. I cannot remember being this happy ever again.

We were swimming together nearly fifty years ago. A tiny child, I wore a blue swimsuit with ruching on the front. You wore green and white trunks. You used those shorts again years later, when we swam in Italian waters, seas as warm as a blanket.

Our mother gasps when she is surprised by a large wave. You capture the moment on your super 8 movie camera.

Later we rewound the film and saw her again, backwards and forwards. She didn't mind when we laughed.

You owned the same shorts when I was older, though the opportunities to swim were fewer. You didn't like the cold, but that hasn't always been the case.

You swam whenever you found the opportunity as a boy. You splashed around the swimming holes near your home. Your brothers hoisted themselves out of the water when your mother called, but you stayed, hauling your skinny body back and forth through green water. My grandmother stood at the side of the pool with a stick, preparing to whack you when you crawled out. Her face was granite, her voice a storm of insults. Not a great incentive for you to leave, but eventually you climbed over the edge and took what was coming.

You believed in facing the consequences of your actions, and that's something you taught me too.

As a boy you were in and out of the water all the time.

It's August 1941. You are thirteen. Like your brothers, you are passionate about the father of Bengali literature and music. Your hero has died. The streets are thronged with people in mourning. You push your way through the crowds, trying to catch a glimpse of the heart of the event. But you are miles from the centre. You are hemmed in on the banks of the Ganges, the sacred river that lays souls to rest. You find a solution. You dive into the water and swim to a better vantage point.

This was a common theme throughout your life. You found your way across water to a better vantage point. Always moving to a better place.

Sometimes you swam against the current. You went where no one else dared to, your determination both an asset and a weight around your neck. It could isolate you as readily as bring you peace.

You swam away from those you loved. Kept yourself above the taint of lives lived less well than yours.

When you swam back, everyone had left without you.

❖

Let us meet again in a pre-monsoon dawn.

Let crazed winds drive us mad.

Let us dance in circles of joy.

Let us hold hands and laugh at how seriously we took ourselves.

Let us tumble in the water that waits for us all.

Thanks

Eileen Merriman for injecting magic into everything I write.

Nancy Stohlman for teaching me there was more to making a collection or novella-in-flash than throwing everything into a pot and stirring.

Matt Potter for giving me the confidence to attempt putting this work together, and for all his help.

Heather Matthews for believing in me.

Mits and Bob Ghosh for sharing a similar journey, with me, to the one the protagonist experiences in this collection of stories, which are mostly make believe.

Acknowledgements

The following have been previously published:

- 'Bhagubhai's Thumb', *The Quick Brown Dog* – Journal of the Hagley Writers' Institute, (November 2017)
- 'Incomplete Lotus', *Long Exposure Magazine* (October 2016)
- 'Umnath', *Firefly Magazine* (November 2015)
- 'The Thickening of Blood', *Hektoen International* (December 2016)
- 'The Basket', *Fictive Dream* (October 2017)
- 'Heaven Street', *Brilliant Flash Fiction* (March 2017)
- 'Bearwood', *Flash Frontier: An Adventure in Short Fiction* (November 2014)
- 'Harborne High Street', *The Citron Review* (December 2015)
- 'Shadow', *Flash Fiction Magazine* (August 2016)
- 'O', *Flash Fiction Press* (September 2016)
- 'Garden of Eden Park', *Landfall* (November 2015), also shortlisted for Asia New Zealand Foundation short fiction competition (October 2014)

About the Author

Nod Ghosh completed a creative writing course at the Hagley Writers' Institute in Christchurch, New Zealand in 2014. Her stories and poems have appeared in *Landfall*, *Takahē*, *JAAM*, and other New Zealand and overseas publications.

Anthologies featuring Nod's work include: *Horizons2*, *Love on the Road* and *Landmarks* (2015); *Leaving the Red Zone* (2016); *Sleep is A Beautiful Colour*, *True*, and *Wiser* (2017), and *Happy²* (2018).

Nod's competition placements include:
• Runner up New Zealand National Flash Fiction Day, 2016.
• Runner up Bath Flash Fiction award, June 2017.
• Joint 1st place Wallace Foundation Creative Non Fiction Contest, 2018.
• Runner up North and South short short story competition, 2016 and 2018.

Nod was born in the U.K. to Indian parents, and works as a medical laboratory scientist. The day job involves writing the truth, which is why it's such fun writing made up stuff at night.

Visit Nod's website at http://www.nodghosh.com/about/.

Also from TRUTH SERUM PRESS

https://truthserumpress.net/catalogue/

- *Kiss Kiss* by Paul Beckman
  978-1-925536-21-8 (paperback) 978-1-925536-22-5 (eBook)
- *Dollhouse Masquerade* by Samuel E. Cole
  978-1-925536-43-0 (paperback) 978-1-925536-44-7 (eBook)
- *Legs and the Two-Ton Dick* by Melinda Bailey
  978-1-925536-37-9 (paperback) 978-1-925536-38-6 (eBook)

- *On the Bitch* by Matt Potter
  978-1-925536-45-4 (paperback) 978-1-925536-46-1 (eBook)
- *Inklings* by Irene Buckler
  978-1-925536-41-6 (paperback) 978-1-925536-42-3 (eBook)
- *Too Much of the Wrong Thing* by Claire Hopple
  978-1-925536-33-1 (paperback) 978-1-925536-34-8 (eBook)

Also from TRUTH SERUM PRESS and EVERYTIME PRESS

https://truthserumpress.net/catalogue/
https://everytimepress.com/everytime-press-catalogue/

- *Track Tales* by Mercedes Webb-Pullman
  978-1-925536-35-5 (paperback) 978-1-925536-36-2 (eBook)
- *True Truth Serum Vol. 1*
  978-1-925536-29-4 (paperback) 978-1-925536-30-0 (eBook)
- *The In-Betweens* by Davon Loeb
  978-1-925536-56-0 (paperback) 978-1-925536-57-7 (eBook)

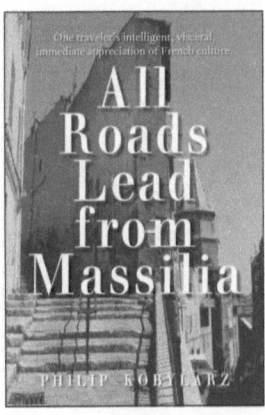  

- *All Roads Lead from Massilia* by Philip Kobylarz
  978-1-925536-27-0 (paperback) 978-1-925536-28-7 (eBook)
- *It's About the Dog* by Guilie Castillo Oriard
  978-1-925536-19-5 (paperback) 978-1-925536-20-1 (eBook)
- *Lenin's Asylum* by A. A. Weiss
  978-1-925536-50-8 (paperback) 978-1-925536-51-5 (eBook)

Also from TRUTH SERUM PRESS and PURE SLUSH BOOKS

https://truthserumpress.net/catalogue/
https://pureslush.com/store/

- *Hello Berlin!* by Jason S. Andrews
  978-1-925536-11-9 (paperback) 978-1-925536-12-6 (eBook)
- *Deer Michigan* by Jack C. Buck
  978-1-925536-25-6 (paperback) 978-1-925536-26-3 (eBook)
- *Rain Check* by Levi Andrew Noe
  978-1-925536-09-6 (paperback) 978-1-925536-10-2 (eBook)

- *Lust 7 Deadly Sins Vol. 1*
  978-1-925536-47-8 (paperback) 978-1-925536-48-5 (eBook)
- *Gluttony 7 Deadly Sins Vol. 2*
  978-1-925536-54-6 (paperback) 978-1-925536-55-3 (eBook)
- *Happy² Pure Slush Vol. 15*
  978-1-925536-39-3 (paperback) 978-1-925536-40-9 (eBook)

www.ingramcontent.com/pod-product-compliance
Lightning Source LLC
Chambersburg PA
CBHW050822180626
46814CB00004B/1410